Halfway Home

10668217

MIDWEST REFLECTIONS

Memoirs and personal histories of the people of the Upper Midwest

Halfway Home

A GRANDDAUGHTER'S BIOGRAPHY

Mary Logue

MINNESOTA HISTORICAL SOCIETY PRESS • ST. PAUL

Midwest Reflections
Memoirs and personal histories of the people of the Upper
Midwest

Minnesota Historical Society Press
St. Paul 55102

Manufactured in the United States of America
10 9 8 7 6 5 4 3 2 1

International Standard Book Number   0-87351-331-2 (cloth)
                                    0-87351-332-0 (paper)

♾ *The paper used in this publication meets the minimum
requirements of the American National Standard for
Information Sciences—Permanence for Printed Library
Materials, ANSI Z39.48-1984.*

Library of Congress Catalog-in-Publication Data
Logue, Mary.
    Halfway home: a granddaughter's biography / Mary Logue.
        p.   cm.
    Includes bibliographical references.
    ISBN 0-87351-331-2 (cloth). — ISBN 0-87351-332-0 (pbk.)
    1. Kirwin, Mae McNally, 1894-1961. 2. Chokio (Minn.)—
Biography. 3. Chokio (Minn.)—Social life and customs.
4. Kirwan family. 5. Logue, Mary—Family. I. Title.
    F614.C46L64 1996
    977.6'42—dc20   92-2641
                                                     CIP

The photograph on page 5 (detail) is by Jet Lowe, Historic
American Engineering Record MN-52-2, National Park Service,
negative in the Library of Congress, Washington, D.C. Images
on p. 16 and 38 are from original documents at the Minnesota
Historical Society. All other photographs are from the collections of the author and her family. "Song in Killeshandra" was
first published in *Discriminating Evidence: Poems* (Denver:
Mid-List Press, 1990).

To my Mother Dear,

Ruthmary Kirwin Logue

(1921-1987)

CONTENTS

CONTENTS

ACKNOWLEDGMENTS

I would never have undertaken this project if it were not for my mother, Ruthmary Kirwin Logue. This book was her idea, and how I wish she were here to read it. I will never forget her stories and songs, her love and support, her sense of herself and her own history. Next to her, my aunt Pat Kirwin Anfinson worked the hardest to make this book happen, answering innumerable questions and making recordings about her childhood in Chokio that provided a framework for much of the book.

Kay McNally Grossman and Joanie Wensman McNally I must thank for many cups of coffee, great stories, and the warmest of welcomes, which made my stays in Chokio real homecomings. Special acknowledgments to Don Eisenmenger, Roni Eisenmenger, Mary Jo Vickoren, Jim Eisenmenger, Kathy Kirwin, Hugh Anfinson, Tead Kirwin, Donna Reichmuth, and all my other Kirwin relatives for sharing their reminiscences about Mae with me and for creating a family in which stories were told and honored.

For hours of reading and questions that made me dig deeper, I thank James Rogers, Lawrence Sutin, Mary Hinderlie, R. D. Zimmerman, and my sisters, Robin and Dodie Logue.

I have been especially fortunate to have a Wednesday night writing crew—Becky Bohan, Deborah Woodworth, Charles Buckman-Ellis, Tom Rucker, Marilyn Bos, George Sorenson, now of Los Angeles, and Andrew Hinderlie, now of New Orleans—who have helped me for over five years, with this book and many others.

A big thanks to Deborah Miller, head of the Minnesota Historical Society's Research Department, which supported my research on this book with a grant; to Ann Regan and Deborah Swanson of the Minnesota Historical Society Press, who with freelance editor Jan Grover led me safely through the labyrinth of putting the manuscript together; and to Jean Brookins, the society's Assistant Director for Publications and Research, who encouraged me from the beginning and cheered me on along the way.

To all the librarians and research assistants in all the places I searched for information, particularly at the Minnesota History Center, Blue Earth Historical Society, and Minneapolis Public Library: I bless you for your help and patience. I know I could get snippy when I was trying to find something.

I owe a special debt to Larry Hutchings, curator, and Tami K. Plank, research assistant, at the Stevens County Historical Society for finding information that I didn't even know existed. Thanks to Dr. William Friedrich, for his analysis of my great-aunt Irene McNally's medical records. Thanks to the people of Chokio, past and present, including Ann Dorweiler, Chuck Grossman, and Marvin Leuthardt.

Love and thanks to Peter Hautman, who has learned more about my family than he ever dreamed he would.

My final note of acknowledgment must go to Mae McNally Kirwin for being a woman her granddaughter will never forget.

A word on the text: many of the quotations in this book are taken from early Minnesota newspapers, and there are a profusion of misspellings and typos, some of them good fun. Rather than litter the quotations with *sic*s, I have chosen to reproduce them as they originally appeared.

PROLOGUE

My grandmother, Mae Kirwin, scared me. She had blunt-cut gray hair that bristled like a coarse brush; her voice was deep and loud; she spoke her mind; and I never knew what she was going to do next. She didn't read me books or bake me cookies. The one lovely memory I have of her is when she showed me how to make a doll out of a hollyhock blossom. One summer day, she picked a blossom from the huge red and pink hollyhocks growing along the south side of her white clapboard house, turned it upside down, and it danced in the breeze for me, transformed into a doll with a flower-petal gown. My grandmother died when I was nine. She was sixty-seven. I've wondered ever since who she was.

The year before my mother died, she spent much of her time worrying about my grandmother. She was afraid that when she herself was gone, no one would be left to remember Mae. So my mother, Ruthmary Kirwin Logue, decided that I should write a book about my grandmother. She made notes for this book. She got out photographs and showed them to me, naming all the people in them. She and her sister Pat Anfinson taped conversations about growing up with my grandmother.

But I didn't want to write a book about Mae. I was too worried about my own mother. After all, she was dying.

It had always saddened my mother that I hadn't known

her mother better. In fact, I was the only child in my family who remembered Mae at all. My younger sister Robin was only two years old when Mae died and Dodie had not yet been born.

One day at the end of winter in St. Paul, my mother and I circled Dayton's Bluff on the freeway. Melting snow smeared all the cars with slush. My mother said, "You know, your grandma Kirwin wasn't really a good grandmother for little kids. You would have liked her a lot better as you got older." Her voice choked up and she stared out the dirty car windows. I tried to assure her that I thought fondly of her mother, but I wasn't very convincing.

I have few memories of my grandmother and some of them are just snippets: I remember her ironing in the kitchen in our old house, her voice booming out at my mother; running to the neighbor's to get me a hat so I could go to Mass on Sunday; and plucking chickens with me over a garbage barrel after singeing off the feathers. Mae never owned a conventional car, but in her later years, she needed some way to get around town for her groceries and errands, so her kids bought her an electric car that could go about seven miles on a charge. I was enchanted with her electric car.

The two strongest memories that form my impression of Mae Kirwin are both unpleasant. One summer when I was probably seven or eight, I was sent to stay with her. That was the visit when my older cousin Mary Jo informed me that I wouldn't go to heaven since I was being raised Lutheran and everyone knew there was only enough room in heaven for Catholics. It was the summer when my other cousin Roni taught me how to speak Pig Latin as we slept together in the big bed in the front room with the soft summer wind stirring the curtains.

Before my cousins showed up, I was lonely and cried myself to sleep every night, my head stuffed into my pillow so my grandma wouldn't hear me and feel bad. Then an old relative died and I heard my parents were coming out for the funeral. I was so happy—they could take me home. While we awaited their arrival, Grandma and I went to the grocery store in town. On one of the swivel racks, I discovered a book of fairy tales with a golden binding and wonderful full-color pictures. When I let my grandmother know that I wanted to go back home with my parents, she promised me that if I stayed, she would buy me that book. So I stayed, but she forgot her promise. I never reminded her, and I never got the book.

During the same visit, Grandmother was doing laundry in the basement and had left something on the stove. I sat in the dining room, looking at the newspaper, trying to make a paper doll out of the model in a clothing ad. I was tracing her, very involved in my work. My grandmother clomped up the stairs with a load of wash and started yelling. I poked my head into the kitchen and saw that a dishtowel hanging over the stove had caught on fire and gone up in flames, scorching the wall. My grandmother tried furiously to put it out and once she had, she turned on me and screamed: What had I been doing? Why hadn't I smelled the fire? I stood still, too terrified to say anything. Later, when I made it home, I told my mother about the fire. She explained to me that Grandma had been scared, that she had yelled at me because she loved me. But that explanation never made much sense.

It has been five years since my mother died and I'm worried that she will be forgotten. But I've come to see that there is an order in which such histories should be undertaken. I'm finally ready to write the story of my grandmother's life— a story about growing up Irish Catholic in western Minnesota, about the power of the wind on the wide prairies and how a family fought to stay together through the Depression. But mostly it's about Mae McNally Kirwin, the short, stocky woman who raised my mother.

Claiming Chokio
1840-1890

. . . seek alone to hear the strange things said

By God to the bright hearts of those long dead,

and learn to chaunt a tongue men do not know.

Come near; I would, before my time to go,

Sing of old Eire and the ancient ways:

Red Rose, proud Rose, sad Rose of all my days.

W. B. Yeats
"To the Rose upon the Rood of Time"

Overleaf: Grain elevators, Chokio, 1990

Claiming Chokio
1840-1890

. . . seek alone to hear the strange things said

By God to the bright hearts of those long dead,

and learn to chaunt a tongue men do not know.

Come near; I would, before my time to go,

Sing of old Eire and the ancient ways:

Red Rose, proud Rose, sad Rose of all my days.

W. B. Yeats
"To the Rose upon the Rood of Time"

Overleaf: Grain elevators, Chokio, 1990

now want to claim Chokio.

In elementary school, when my third-grade teacher asked us what nationality we were, we knew what she meant. Hands flew in the air as we acknowledged our heritage—part German, part Swedish, part Ojibway, part Irish. All of our ancestors had come from another country or another culture, and we claimed them as a way to define ourselves.

However, I knew that both of my parents were born in small, rural Minnesota towns—my father in Waseca, my mother in Chokio—and that these towns held their own power. Both had Indian names; both were a fair drive from where we lived in St. Paul. And even though I could still hear an Irish lilt in my mother's voice, the stronger sound was the pull of the Dakota winds coming down the Red River Valley, lengthening her vowels, snapping her consonants.

Chokio, I even liked saying it when I was young. I wondered what the word meant. I remember when I was seven and my mother made a phone call to my grandmother Mae. When the phone bill came, she had been charged for a call to Chicago, not Chokio. My mother laughed at the mistake. I bristled at this, slightly outraged that the operator didn't recognize the name of my mother's hometown.

Even now, when people ask me where my grandmother Kirwin was from, I locate Chokio for any Minnesotan, with,

I am sure, a tone of voice that implies they should know where it is. "It's in the bump on the west side of the state," I say. "You know, where the Red River starts flowing north and the Minnesota starts south."

⬥

I was nine and a half when my family drove out to Chokio after my grandmother's funeral to pick up my aunt Dutt, Mom's sister, and some of my grandmother's furniture. My father drove a green '56 Chevy and pulled a trailer. I don't remember much about Mae's house being emptied out, but I knew enough to be quiet and to tend to the little kids. No one was in a good mood. My mom was horridly sad and my father yelled at the slightest mistake.

My parents loaded up the trailer and set off back to St. Paul as night fell and fog rolled across the prairies. My father didn't realize that the weight of the trailer pulled the back of the car down and allowed the fuel gauge to read fuller than it was. We ran out of gas and sat in the car while my father hitched a ride to the nearest town to get help. A sad and ignoble journey, emptying Chokio of all that tied me to it, I thought.

With my grandmother dead, I figured I had no reason to go back to Chokio. My mother went to visit some McNally cousins, but they were only names to me. Chokio was on the other side of the state, not on the way to anyplace.

But when I was in my mid-twenties, I was asked to do a reading with the group Poets Outloud, which had received a grant to do a series of readings in Morris, only fifteen miles away from Chokio. I invited my mother to go with me. We visited the Catholic elementary school and, later, a senior home in Morris. My mother mentioned to the old women seated in chairs in the lounge that she was Mae Kirwin's daughter and I, her granddaughter. Heads nodded and fingers unfolded as memory moved across their faces. They smiled. One woman said her name, "Mae Kirwin, sure, I remember her. She ran the post office. She was a good woman." High praise in those parts.

A few years later, I used my local connection to break the ice when I taught writing in senior centers around Alexandria, or "Alec," as it was known to nearby communities, which included Chokio. When I mentioned that my grandmother was from Chokio, I became one of them, one of their own, not some visiting writer from the big cities, but a woman with ties to the country they had lived in all their lives. Maybe I would understand what they had to say, what they would write about. Chokio gave me an entrance into their lives, and I used it.

⁕

Driving toward Chokio from the Twin Cities, midsummer of 1993, seventy degrees out. The land settles flat like a wrinkled cloth that is stretched out to the Minnesota–South Dakota border. Clover and mustard line Highway 28, growing in the ditches alongside the fields of alfalfa and sickly corn. With all the rain, the land cups water wherever there is a hollow. Looking out over the countryside, I can't help but see the similarity to the plain, pieced quilts women made from bits of fabric. The land seems sewn with its patterned fields of wheat and sorghum.

West of Morris, the earth is wet. A cloudburst the previous week had poured down more than seven inches of water in two hours and the ground just hasn't been able to absorb it yet. I have always thought of this part of the state as dry and dusty, but this year it is green and glimmering with pool after pool of water where cornfields should be.

As I drive into town, it is easy for me to see that Chokio was built on a slough. Water everywhere. The ditch north of town filled during the storm so a hole was dug through the road bed to widen a culvert and drain the town. People had geysers of sewage shooting out of their toilets. Most managed to clean up their basements, but the fields are another matter. It is well after the Fourth of July, but the corn is stunted at ankle height. Businesses in Chokio are hurting. Hard to believe that only a few years ago, we went through two years of bad drought. Farmers here haven't recovered from that.

Minnesota is dotted with these small towns, grown closer together in the mid- to late-nineteenth century than they need to be today. Demographers generally refer to towns with fewer than 1,000 inhabitants as "small cities." In 1990 there were 539 such small towns in Minnesota. On that stretch of road from Morris to Brown's Valley, there's a town about every six miles. Most of them are having a hard time surviving.

The problem isn't a significant loss of population in these towns. Rather, no one uses their main streets anymore. It takes people fifteen minutes to drive to Morris, so they don't need to shop in Chokio. For a shopping spree, they drive to the K-Mart in Alec or to the mall in St. Cloud. In 1984, the *Wall Street Journal* quoted a sociologist who predicted that the prospects for a town with a population under 1,000 surviving were low. The 1990 U.S. census found that there were 521 people living in Chokio.

The train only stops in Chokio now if the grain elevator company requests a pickup. The old depot has been moved and is being used to store machinery. A few businesses remain: a grocery store, a post office, a cafe, a clothing store, a bank, and my favorite—a shop that is owned by my relative Kay Grossman—a tanning booth, balloon shop, Avon cosmetics, and used bookstore, all in one.

There is no real reason for people to go to Chokio anymore unless they were born there or have relatives still living there. There is no lake; all the sloughs were drained to build farmland. Farming is the only real business, and if the farmers have a tough year like the last few, everyone in town suffers. In 1925, Stevens County claimed 1,299 farms with an average of 257 acres. In 1987, only 619 farms dotted the land, but the average acreage had shot up to 477.

One weekend a year the town booms. On the opening day of pheasant season, relatives and hunters crowd the town, filling the spare bedrooms and going out to hunt in the dried cornfields. Oddly enough, the pheasants themselves are immigrants. Brought from China in the last century, they proceeded to push out the prairie chickens. Today they too are on the decline.

⌖

Digging through the library in Morris, I came across a map of Stevens County from 1874, six years before my ancestors made their way across Minnesota to farm there. On the eastern side of the county, there's a dot for Morris and a few farms are noted, but west of Morris there's nothing—no lakes are named, no towns are founded, no homesteads are claimed. A double line runs across the map north of Baker Township marked the "Morris & Sissiton Agency Road." I can tell from this map where my great-grandfather Peter McNally's farm will be because his slough is clearly marked.

In my drives around the countryside, I have tried to see the land as it must have appeared to the pioneers, but the telephone lines and poles, the tree clumps sheltering farms, the plowed and neatly sown fields, even the road itself establish a kind of order on the land. The hand of man is strong, and it's hard to look beyond it.

So, thank goodness, an eighth-grade girl named Emma Peterson wrote an article on the geography and natural history of Stevens County in 1903 as an exercise for her grammar school graduation. In her wonderfully old-fashioned, florid way, she described what the land must have looked like in 1864 when the first European settlers came to it:

> The land is a gently rolling prairie of a rich loamy soil peculiarly adapted to the cultivation and production of all cereals. The yields of small grains are abundant and the markets are some of the best. The county is situated on the table land of the state, 1500 feet above sea level and near where the Red River of the North, the Minnesota, and Mississippi rivers take their source. . . .
>
> In the first years of settlement buffaloes were seen roving around the prairies east of the Pomme de Terre River. Elk, deer and lynx were numerous, and bear were also seen at a few places. Large eagles' nests then adorned many of the largest trees surrounding the lake shores. Cormorants, swans, and pelicans resorted regularly every summer to the larger lakes, but rabbits and prairie chickens were then very scarce.

I have seen the pelicans she describes. On my last trip out to Chokio, before I got to Morris, I saw a flock of pelicans lift into the air and start their characteristic circling. In an ever widening gyre, as Yeats might say, they spiraled up into the sky until they were dots in the blue and I drove beneath them and on to town.

Emma went on to tell about the weather, always a major concern of Minnesotans, especially of farmers.

> The people who came in the early days of Morris had very hard times, for the weather was intensely cold in winter, there being no woods or buildings to prevent the terrible north wind from coming down upon the poor lone settlers. The weather would be so very cold that for seventeen days in succession the thermometer would only be 28 degrees below zero for the warmest, and 42 degrees below zero for the coldest. The summers are just about the same, with only a few changes. But the cultivation of the land has made

them much cooler, for before then the climate was almost desert like.

Toward the end of her piece, Emma wrote about the grasshopper plagues, a phenomenon that happens cyclically every twenty years or so. Emma described the grasshoppers poetically:

> They would come down just like rain and so many of them would get on one stalk of corn that it would bend it clear over to the ground. The hoppers were much worse on the other side of the river than on this side: although the hoppers were so many and ate everything green, they made a very pretty picture as they descended down from the sky. They resembled large snow flakes, as their large white wings were the only parts of them to be seen.

However, she quoted a local newspaper from 1876 that viewed the grasshoppers differently:

> The grasshoppers are now thicker here than ever before; a perfect cloud of them rise up before one where ever foot is set on prairie, road or side walk. As they whack against the office roof and window glass not a foot from the type we are now setting, and we literally move in an atmosphere of grasshoppers. The wheat is nearly all too ripe for them to destroy much, but God help the owners of the green fields. There is no use disguising the fact that this part of Minnesota has the blues this holy Sabbath day.

At the close of her essay, Emma praised the early settlers: "All these circumstances proved too much for many a man and woman that lacked true womanhood and true manhood."

I was so relieved that my ancestors had stuck it out.

⟡

Chokio exists because of the Wadsworth Trail. Legend has it that the trail was an old Dakota and Mandan path that the tribes took when they came down the Red River to Lake Traverse and then traveled east. Later it was used by the U.S. government supply trains and soldiers going from St. Cloud to Fort Wadsworth near Sisseton, South Dakota. Three well-known stopping places lay along its route in Stevens County; the Chokio station and its Half-way House was one of them. Remnants of the trail remain to this day. A sword was found stuck into the ground along the trail, indicating a soldier had been buried there. A payroll load of gold en route to the fort was rumored to have been buried in Morris Township. After the soldiers came through, settlers used the trail to immigrate into Stevens County.

A small trading post and some outbuildings were built at the Half-way House, which is actually half a mile north of present-day Chokio. Mrs. Hamin, an English woman, worked at the relay station, which became Chokio.

The origin of this name is unclear. In *Chokio Community History,* Ervy Townsend, whose grandmother worked at the Half-way House, recounted the story:

> According to my Dad, his mother cooked at the "Half-way House" north of Chokio on the old Wadsworth Trail. When the railroad was built the trainmen asked her to put a name on the shelter or depot. She had a faithful Indian lad who had worked hard for her at the Half-way House, his name was "Kok hi oh." He died while in her employ so she asked that it be named for him. It was finally pronounced "Chokio." Several years ago, I inquired of a Sioux Indian as to the meaning of the word Chokio. As close as he could come from our spelling, he said it meant a "resting place, half-way or part-way."

When I looked up the word in *Grammar and Dictionary of the Dakota Language,* the closest word I found was *ćokaya,* which means "middle or in the middle." The "ć" sound was pronounced like the "ch" in *chin.* Older people in Chokio pronounced the town's name with that hard "ch" sound, while most people today pronounce it like *Chicago*.

The railroad came to Morris in 1871. Then in 1880 the St. Paul & Pacific Railroad Company tracks were laid from Morris out to Brown's Valley, half a mile south of the Wadsworth Trail. The settlement moved. The first dwelling was the Flambo House, which offered a place to stay for travelers and drinking and gambling for all. Early postal records refer to the town as Chokaga.

The first postmaster was Mrs. Maria Clark, appointed on November 10, 1879. The post office was discontinued on April 7, 1881, and re-established on November 5, 1891. James H. McNally, my grandmother's uncle, was appointed postmaster. The McNally family continued to hold important positions at the post office in Chokio for the next hundred years.

My grandmother's father's family, the McNallys, and the early history of Chokio are intertwined. In late 1882, John McNally, Sr., my great-great-grandfather, along with thirty-one others, petitioned the state to organize the township. The first meeting was held at his home. His eldest son William was elected clerk, and he and his namesake John were elected supervisors.

When I was in Chokio doing research on this book, I drove out into the country to find the old homestead. The roads lie straight on the flat land and cross each other at the mile mark. They follow the plat book and some of them are unnavigable in bad weather, just two rut marks through the fields. Even in a car, the movement over this land seems slow. I tried to imagine what it must have felt like to be settled into a house with only a few trees planted, miles from the train station and from the small grouping of buildings people were calling a town.

Plat map of Baker Township, Stevens County, Minnesota, 1910

I sat in my car and looked at the small clapboard house that was the original Pete McNally farm. The land can't have changed that much. But what a difference from the country of my ancestors. Ireland is a rolling, stony country where it can be hard to find a plot of land worth sowing a few seeds in. But it is a green country. Here, for half the year the flat land is blanketed with snow and for a good chunk of the other half it turns golden in the summer sun. What had the Irish immigrants thought of this place?

I think often of my Irish blood. My mother was three-quarters Irish—all of those ancestors had come over from Ireland during the potato famine. She was raised in a community where the Irish stuck together. Irish words peppered her vocabulary. When I was a child, I didn't notice them. They were just the way my mother spoke. But when a manuscript of mine was copyedited and the editor queried a word I had written, saying "This word has no such meaning," I was puzzled. The word was *skiff.* I had written "a skiff of snow." I knew what the word meant. My mother had used it often. So I looked it up in my small *Webster's* dictionary, where it was defined as a small boat. Well, I had heard that sense of it, but it wasn't the way I was using the word. I kept looking. Finally, in a large dictionary, I found my word and the definition I sought: "skiff: a thin covering," which was of Gaelic origin. When my mother said the word, she would often rub her fingers together to show how thin this covering was.

So I decided to hunt for these Irish words. I knew there were more of them hidden in my speech. Some of them, like *hooligan,* have entered into American usage, but another that had not was a word my mother used often when one of her daughters wasn't fixed up as nicely as she thought she should be. She would call her "a streel." Again, I knew what it meant—a woman who didn't keep herself up. Not complimentary at all. And I couldn't find the word in any dictionary. Then I read the word in a recent book by Rosemary Mahoney, *Whoredom in Kimmage: Irish Women Coming of Age*. An Aran Islander said of Nancy Sinatra, "She was a nasty little streel." My mother would have agreed. Mahoney went on to explain, "A streel, I knew, was a slatternly woman."

Maybe because I'm a writer, these words link me strongly to a small country that my grandmother never saw but that she was probably reminded of every day of her life. After all, her grandparents remembered the country well. They were all in their twenties when they left it.

The McNally family was headed by John and Bridget Mullen McNally. Both of them were born in Ireland within a few years of each other. However, I could find no mention of where or when. Different dates were given for their births on various documents; their death certificates list John's year of birth as 1823 and Bridget's as 1827. Bridget's parents were known to be Thomas Mullen and Bridget Campbell, but John said nothing of his ancestors. He would not talk of Ireland, and the only mention he made of leaving that country was to tell of the boat trip to America, when he remembered cinders from the boat's smokestack singeing his face.

This amnesia about Ireland was not uncommon among the Irish famine immigrants. According to sociologist Andrew M. Greeley, "The American Irish made it by forgetting their past and trying to be like everyone else."

It is hard to know where the two Irish immigrants John and Bridget met; they might have known each other in Ireland. In the 1900 Minnesota census, they both gave 1849 as the date of their immigration, one year after the second severe potato blight in Ireland.

⌘

How integral the history of the potato is to my family. Ironically, the potato came from the Americas and, once established in Europe, sent my ancestors fleeing to North America. Native to South America, the potato was probably introduced into Europe in the sixteenth century. By the mid-seventeenth century, it was grown in England as a food crop.

In the eighteenth century, Ireland shifted from pastoral to tillage farming and the land continued to be divided up. A nourishing, economical vegetable, the potato was adopted as the principal food. A six-member family could live off of the produce from an acre and a half of land. Thanks to the potato, the population increased and dependence on it continued to grow.

In 1842 and 1844, a potato blight hit the eastern United States, but because so many other foods were available there, the loss of the potato wasn't that important. Then the blight traveled to the Continent. In the fall of 1845, it hit Ireland, starting in the southern counties of Waterford and Wexford. Soon the blight covered half the island.

Phytophthora infestans is a fungus, also called late blight. It attacks the leaves and stems of the potato plant, reducing the size of the tuber. A tuber can be infected when it's harvested and then rot in storage, spoiling all the potatoes around it. A family might think they had a large supply of potatoes stored for winter, only to find that the entire batch was rotten. No one knew what to do about the blight. People tried to eat the spoiled potatoes anyway, but they stunk and were putrid. An agricultural bulletin described the devastation: "A field showing but slight infection may in a few days look as if it had been swept by fire or frost."

After a people had been so let down by the potato, you might think they would come to despise it. But the Irish blamed the English for their plight, probably not wrongly so, and kept the potato near and dear. In my family, the potato still reigned supreme as the food most often served at a meal.

For Saturday lunch, my mother often cooked a dish she had learned from her mother—potato soup. So simple. Cut up four boiling potatoes and an onion or two. Boil in lightly salted water for thirty minutes, or until soft. Drain off most of the water. Lightly mash the potatoes, leaving some chunks. Then add a cup of milk and a blob of butter and bring nearly to boil. Serve with fresh pepper sprinkled on top in a big white bowl. I learned this recipe by watching my mother make the soup; it was never written down. I make it often in early fall when the potatoes are new and frost is upon us.

In *The Famine Immigrants,* a set of volumes listing the "Customs Passenger Lists" for immigrants from Ireland landing in the port of New York from 1846 to 1851, I tried to find my great-great-grandmother and great-great-grandfather. I looked for John McNally, John Nallen, Bridget Mullen, and Bridget McNally (just in case they had been married in Ireland). I found many people with those names leaving Ireland, but no Nallens at all. I felt a sorrow looking at the lists of people streaming out of their native land—all the Irish names I've ever known: Malloy, Connor, O'Brien, and even a few Logues leaving from Liverpool or Dublin or Galway.

They left behind a country in dire trouble from both the famine and the diseases that accompanied it—typhus, dysentery, and hunger edema—and a fierce, cold winter.

Because of the land laws of English rule, Catholics in Ireland owned little property and were not allowed to hold important positions. Most Irishmen worked as tenant farmers or "cottiers," as they were called, usually renting less than five acres of land.

In County Cork, one parish lost a quarter of its population during a twelve-month period in 1847–48 to disease and famine. To put this in perspective, Ireland is about one-third the size of Minnesota. In 1990, there were not quite 4.5 million people living in Minnesota. By contrast, in 1841 there were nearly 8.5 million people in Ireland. By 1851, Ireland's population had dropped to 6.5 million. One way or another, people were leaving Ireland.

In those ten years, Ireland lost 2 million people—half to emigration and half to disease. In 1849–50, when my great-great-grandparents left, over 200,000 Irish immigrated to America. Most of the emigration was from the north central and northwest of Ireland, which includes Galway. By 1990, the population of Ireland had dwindled to 3.5 million.

How much to blame the English for the devastation of the potato famine continues to be a controversial question. My Irish blood and sympathies have always made me assume the English were to blame. Two facts jumped out at me when I was reading the arguments of both sides. The first was a description by Charles Trevelyan, the English assistant secretary of the treasury responsible for famine relief, of the famine as a "cure" for the problem of overpopulation: "the direct stroke of an all-wise Providence in a manner as unexpected and as unthought of as it is likely to be effectual." The second was the amount of money that England spent on famine relief—9.5 million pounds—compared to 70 million pounds spent on the futile war in the Crimea.

Individuals were given the money to emigrate in one of two ways: either a landowner paid them to leave so as to be rid of them or a relative sent them remittance money from America. The cost for the boat trip in 1849 was three to four pounds, about one-half to one-third of the annual earnings of a pre-Famine Irish laborer.

The trip was long and hard. Ships were filled to the deck, averaging three hundred to four hundred passengers. These boats were called coffin ships by many. The shortest trips took forty days. Even though the passengers had been promised an allowance of flour, rice, oatmeal, tea, sugar, and water every week, there was often not enough to go around. Besides hunger and disease, fighting and stealing were common on the ships. Although mortality had declined—thirty years earlier, nearly one-fifth of passengers had died during the crossings—the trip still took its toll.

Bridget was close to twenty-two years old and John probably twenty-six. In the ship's records, I found a twenty-three-year-old Bridget Mullen traveling with a twenty-year-old Bernard; they left Liverpool and arrived in New York City on May 23, 1849. And I found a twenty-six-year-old John McNally who left Dublin and arrived in New York City on May 7, 1849, with a brother, twenty-four-year-old Patrick.

My ancestors were not coming to a country that welcomed them with open arms. Signs in New York and Philadelphia announced "No Irish Need Apply" for jobs. With the huge influx of famine immigrants into the major port cities, there were reports of the Irish begging on the streets.

Two things most Irish immigrants brought with them, even when they lost all their luggage on the trip over, were their Catholic religion and their desire for land.

⧝

A document transcribed in the McNally family papers states that a John Nallen received his citizenship in Pennsylvania on December 9, 1854. John Nallen renounced his allegiance to Queen Victoria and pledged allegiance to the United States. A C. H. Sweeny and an M. M. Morris testified that this Nallen had been in the United States for five years, which agrees with his known immigration date, and in Pennsylvania for a year.

How his name got changed to Nallen is unknown. My guess is that his name was originally McNally (this theory is supported by the fact that there were no Nallens leaving Ireland in 1849 or any years around it) and that he changed it in this country to sound less Irish, but that when he settled on his own land, he changed it back to McNally. But that is just a theory.

The first child born to John and Bridget was a girl, and they named her Mary. She died before she was a year old. Then followed a stream of ten boys and one more girl. Family legend has it that John worked for the railroad. The family moved to Emerald and Erin Prairie townships, Wisconsin, sometime between 1855 and 1857. Then, in 1880, the family moved by oxen to western Minnesota, staking land claims on 480 acres in Stevens County.

One question that occurred to me in charting their travels is why did they continue to move? Why didn't they stay in Wisconsin? After all, by 1880 they were in their fifties, an age at which most people stay put. I attribute their move to the Irish desire for land: they had such a strong sense that if they owned land, they would be all right, no matter what happened around them. Western Minnesota was still seen as the frontier, a place where there was plenty of opportunity. With Bishop John Ireland establishing Catholic parishes in Graceville and Avoca, they didn't need to worry about losing the Church. So they went.

They chose a good time to move to western Minnesota. According to James P. Shannon, who wrote about the Irish immigration into this area, "They came into the West just as the railroads arrived, purchased virgin land at minimal prices, were given all the advantages of a lenient credit sys-

Mae's paternal grandparents, John and Bridget Mullen McNally, with eight of their children, 1898. Standing: Peter, Michael, Patrick, Francis, and James; seated: John, John, Sr., Bridget, and William; kneeling: Joseph and Mary.

tem, and in general enjoyed a bull market for their main crop during their first decade on the prairie."

The 1880 census for Stevens County was done on June 5 and 7 by enumerator Wm. W. Learned, who had a very lovely, even hand with beautiful trills and scrolls, especially on the J's and P's. The twenty-first listing in Baker Township was the whole McNally family, though here the family name was spelled *McNalley* (which is closer to Nallen). It listed John McNalley as a white, male fifty-year-old farmer. His wife Bridget was forty-eight. These ages were probably not correct. William, the oldest son, was twenty-eight, and the rest of the boys followed with only two-year gaps between them: Thomas, John, James, Patrick, Michael, Francis, Peter, and then the only girl, Mary, who was ten. Two more boys followed: Edward, seven, and Joseph, five. My great-grandfather Peter was just thirteen.

The Homestead Act of 1862 gave settlers the right to claim 160 acres. After living on the land for five years and putting in $500 in improvements, the property was theirs to keep. John and four of his sons claimed land—all of Section 26, three miles south and a half mile east of Chokio. Pete McNally claimed another 160 acres of land two miles west of the original family claim. But eventually most of the family moved into town. Pat McNally built the second house in the new town of Chokio.

A family portrait taken in Morris in the 1890s shows a group of handsome men and placid-faced women. By this time two more of the children were missing. Tom went out west, eventually settling in Hoghiam, Washington, and Edward died in 1892.

At that same sitting, a picture was taken of John and Bridget alone. They were both dressed in dark clothes. John wore a suit with a waistcoat and a crooked bow tie. Bridget wore a heavy dress with gathered sleeves and a very full skirt. She was seated in a lovely wicker chair. A worn oriental rug lay at their feet, but surely they were photographed in a photographer's studio. John had a full beard of white hair, but nicely trimmed; Bridget's hair was still dark and worn back in a low bun at her neck. They have the dazed look so common when people are forced to sit too long in one position. I am glad to see them. They were in their late sixties and their children were doing well. They had settled onto their own land and they would die there.

Bridget died first in 1909. Somehow, that doesn't surprise me, for she had borne twelve children, which must have taken a toll on her body. The local newspaper noted that she died at home in Chokio "from infirmities of old age," but the death certificate listed cause of death as "softening of the brain" and the secondary cause as "Old Age." In the church records from St. Mary's, I found that she died at age eighty-two and was given "sacris refecta" or last rites. By this time, two more of their children had died in Chokio—Joe and Mary.

From family papers, I read of the funeral. "Several daughters-in-law made the brown shroud Grandma McNally was buried in. . . . This garment was made at our house and the girls got carried away, liturgically, and made a brown piece about 8" by 12" banded with white satin ribbon and the letters I.H.S. of white ribbon sewed on this. This addition was placed on her chest and she was buried in this."

John McNally died nearly ten years later, in August 1918. Ninety-five years old. He must have done something right. The local paper called him "one of [the] Prosperous Pioneer Farmers of Stevens County. . . . Mr. McNally was the pioneer farmer of the best type and every year of his long residence here added to the respect and admiration accorded him by his large number of friends. He took a large farm when he came here and stuck to it for many years. He was industrious and his industry brot prosperity and he grew with the new country that he helped so much to build up."

His sons were doing well. Most of them had moved into the town of Chokio and married Irish women: Mary McDonnell and Margaret Flynn and Ellen Connors and Agnes Kelly and Loretta Bowen and Mary Griffith and an Honora Reardon. The Reardon is my great-grandmother. She married Peter H. McNally in 1891.

I know less of the Reardons—they were not spoken of much in my family, probably because they lived in the next county over from Chokio. According to their obituaries in the *Graceville Enterprise,* my great-great-grandfather Patrick Reardon was born in County Kerry, in 1834, the son of William Reardon and Mary Dillen or Dillon. Honora was born in County Limerick on January 6, 1837. She was the daughter of William Murphy and Honora Lumey. They both left Ireland in 1861 and married the same year. It is not clear in what order these two events happened.

According to the research my cousin Don Eisenmenger has done, it is probable that the two lived quite close to each other in Ireland:

> Maps recording the distribution of familys with the names of Reardon and Murphy for the two counties involved show a significant overlap of the names. The names also fail to appear in areas of the counties except near the border where both names are frequent. It is likely that both were born within 20 miles of the border shared by the two counties.

I had been told that they lived near Graceville, but I located the family living in the township of Baker in Stevens County in the census of 1885. The father and mother were recorded as Patrick and Hannah, as Honora was called, and they were fifty and forty-five. Six children were living with them then, but Hannah's obituary says she had eight. In 1885, Mary was 20, Billy 17, Michael 15, Nanny (my great-grandmother, also named Honora) 13, Patrick 11, and James 6. It may have been during this time that Nanny and Peter met. He would have been eighteen.

The Reardon family then moved to Malta Township and farmed on a quarter section of land. In 1903, the older Reardons moved into the town of Graceville. Patrick died on March 18, 1908, of a sudden illness, leaving an estate worth $5,405, which consisted of his property in Graceville and the old homestead. The *Graceville Enterprise* called him one of the early pioneers, a man "whose undaunted courage and unflagging industry so successfully surmounted the arduous difficulties and privations incident to the settlement of a new country."

Hannah survived for quite some time, outliving her daughter Nanny, my great-grandmother, and was adjudged incompetent to manage her property in March 1925; she died that September. Again, the local paper had nothing but praise: "So passes another pioneer of the days of struggle and hardship to whom Christian faith was a tower of strength

Mae's father, Peter H. McNally, March 19, 1890

South Saint Paul Library
Checkout Receipt
www.ssplibrary.org
Phone Renewals: 651-450-2999

Title: Halfway home : a granddaughter's biography
Item ID: 32098001666151
Date due: 1/27/2021,23:59

You are responsible for all materials borrowed. Please report all lost cards.

.

.

DAILY FINES ACCRUE ON ALL
OVERDUE ITEMS

.

.

.

Library service will be stopped when unpaid fees and/or fines reach $25 for adults and $10 for children.

.

.

.

.

.

*Mae's mother,
Honora Reardon, n.d.*

and whose ennobling characteristics as a wife and mother made her life possess all the sweetness of a benediction." By the time of her death, only three of Hannah's children were still alive—Mary, William, and Michael.

Michael died in 1951. He and his wife Anna were buried with their daughter Norah in the Catholic cemetery in Chokio; their graves are close to Honora McNally's family plot. I get odd comfort from this, the families mingling in death.

❧

A year after I started my research on Mae McNally Kirwin and family, I drove out to Chokio again. It was 1994, the year my grandmother Mae would have been one hundred. I had studied this town and one of its largest families so intensely that I felt as if I had come back to a second home.

I was housed on the third floor of the old banker's house, now owned by Chuck and Kay McNally Grossman, under the eaves in an enormous room that was once a ballroom. The branches of a cottonwood tree swayed outside the floor-to-ceiling windows next to my futon bed as I read over my notes and the scraps of research I had culled that day.

Before we slept, Kay Grossman and I drifted through the streets of Chokio in the cooling summer air, talking about what Chokio was and what it might be. Kay had lived there all her life. Her father Bud was a second cousin to my grandmother Mae; her mother Joanie was my grandmother's best friend in the last years of her life. We are distantly related by blood, Kay and I, but closely related by thought. We wondered about many of the same things—what did the people who lived in Chokio in 1900 think the town would become? What would be left of the town in 2050? A grouping of houses, no businesses left?

On the second day of my visit, I decided to again drive out to the old homestead. I had found yet another plat map, this one from 1910, which showed that Bridget McNally owned a piece of the section. She would have been dead in 1910, but before she died, she had donated a piece of her land to Rural School District #27.

It was a perfect summer day with the temperature in the mid-eighties. I drove down a straight tarred road for three miles south of Chokio. There on the corner sat the old schoolhouse. I pulled off the road onto a small parking area and got out of the car. The white paint on the side of the clapboard building had so faded that the schoolhouse read gray. An old weathered interlocking roof seemed to be holding on, but the building was deep in the embrace of scrub trees that grew up on the north and south sides of it.

The schoolhouse was a one-room building with the doorway on the south and a bank of windows to the west. There was no door, so I walked in, wary of my step, for the wooden floors were rotting through. A swallow flew out as I entered. There was nothing left in the old school but mildewed plaster walls, hanging wires for electric lamps, and birds' nests.

I wished the windows hadn't been boarded over. I would have liked to see the view the children saw every day when they peeked up from their work. The room was large, and I wondered what it must have taken for the teacher to keep the children attentive on a bright spring day or warm on a frigid January morning.

When I was back outside, I walked to a pile of rocks I had noticed near the road. As I made my way through the tall grass, I glimpsed shrub roses, pink flowers in full bloom. These roses inspired me to take from the pile of field stones a hand-sized pink granite rock. I plunked it in the back of my car and thought no more of it until I was back in Minneapolis the next day.

I brought the stone in with all the rest of my research notes and luggage and set it on the kitchen counter. Peter, the man I live with, picked it up and turned it over.

"This looks like an artifact," he said.

"What?"

"Yeah, see how this side has been smoothed. It looks like this stone might have been used to grind corn into meal. See how worn it is."

I held the pink stone in my hand. I had picked it up because it was such a nice size. Some Dakota Indian woman must have thought the same thing. I wrapped my hand around it and turned it over, rubbing it against my palm. I imagined the other hands that had held it, used it. My great-great-grandmother Bridget might have turned it over in her hands and placed it in the rock pile. I carried it upstairs and set it on my writing desk. Against a wall of books, it sat as real as any word I could write down on a page.

I knew then that if Chokio disappeared in a hundred years, there would be much left by this passing of people: twists of metal, planks of graying wood, tin cans, and bits of glass. Someone else would find them and wonder, too.

Scrolling through the Family
1890–1920

The validity of genealogy is not the

assembly of pedigree culminating

smugly in self, but the extension

of the personal beyond the self

through imaginative encounter

with the intimate otherness of

ghosts within the genes.

Michael Coady
"Oven Lane: The Use of Memory"

Overleaf: Mae, 1897

I felt seasick from scrolling through the censuses on the microfilm reader at the Minnesota History Center. Sitting hunched in front of the hulking gray machine, I grew queasy while I worked. The names of past generations, scrawled in the various delicate hands of the census enumerators, sailed past me like swells on a paper ocean. I found Stevens County, then slowed down and watched for *Baker*, the township where Chokio would soon be incorporated. Then I spied my grandmother's name: "McNally, May 1 [year old]."

In 1894, over one hundred years ago, she had been born to Honora and Peter McNally. Her older brother, Hugh, was two. Someone had written her name down, and now I was looking at a picture of it on film through a projector. I believed in her life more than I had a moment earlier. This was such concrete evidence that she had been born and lived in Chokio. I reached up and touched the writing on the screen.

I made a copy of it and tucked it into my folder with the other censuses I had gathered: 1880, the year the McNally family moved to the area; 1885, when the older boys moved out and claimed land of their own. The story of their lives was told on these simple pieces of paper that the government collected to keep track of its people.

I was so happy to have found Mae. Even though I had

already written two mystery novels, I had never felt so much like a detective as I did while sleuthing through public records. Again and again, I was amazed at what information I found and what I could extrapolate from it. For example, looking at her name as it was written on the census, I learned a new bit of information. I had always known my grandmother by the name Mae. But I knew that I was named for her and that her given name was Mary Joseph McNally. From reading the census, I learned that she had been called Mae since birth.

Mae is no longer a common nickname for Mary. When friends or family shorten my name, it's to "Mar," pronounced like the female horse. But to understand why an Irish family would shorten it to Mae, you need to know how the Irish pronounce the name. They say, "Mae-ree," while we Americans now pronounce it, "Mare-ee." So Mae was the first half of the name and very common, as I have found in reading through the old newspapers from turn-of-the-century Chokio. Again, it makes sense: Mary was the most common name given to girls in these Irish-Catholic families, as it was in most of the Western world.

Honora and Peter's first child, Hugh Francis McNally, was born May 4, 1893. Slightly over a year later, Mary Joseph McNally was born on May 15, 1894. Her father was twenty-seven and her mother was twenty-two. A third child, Urban, was born in October 1896, but according to his death record, he died six months later from an obstruction of the bowels. Edna McNally was born in 1898 and Irene in 1901. Irene was born a twin, but her stillborn sister was never given a name.

This death of a twin must have been a very traumatic event for both the mother and her children. Twin research has found that society treats the birth of twins as a special event and that mothers who lose one of their twins often grieve more than women who have lost their only baby. Studies of the surviving twins show that they live with a sense of incompleteness that can make relationships in general difficult, in particular those with the opposite sex. Irene, as I discovered later, certainly had a difficult life.

So within the first six years of her life, my grandmother had lost two siblings. This heartbreaking misfortune continued.

George McNally was born in 1902. In 1909 he had an "Inanition Obstruction of bowels" that lasted ten days and then he died. The death record was signed by B. M. Randall, an M.D. from Graceville.

Olive Marguerite was born in 1905 and was called simply Marguerite. The final baby, Ruth, was born in 1907 and lived for nearly three years, dying of "Intussusception," according to C. L. McCann, the Chokio doctor. This last death must have been especially hard on Mae, who would have been thirteen when the baby was born and might well have adopted Ruth emotionally as her own. Ten years later, my grandmother named her first baby, my mother, for her sister Ruth.

By the time my grandmother was sixteen, she had four living siblings and four who had died. In order, the surviving McNally children were Hugh, Mae, Edna, Irene, and Marguerite.

❧

One wonderful discovery I made while digging through the archives at the History Center was that my great-great-uncle, Charles E. McAllen, started the first newspaper in Chokio in 1897. He called it the *Chokio Times,* and it ran for a year and nine months. I was elated for two reasons:

The Chokio Times, *March 17, 1897*

this newspaper would give me a pinhole view into my ancestors' lives, and I loved the idea of someone distantly related to me, preceding me in writing about this prairie town.

At the time the first issue came out, there were about 150 people living in Chokio. A good number of them—between twenty and thirty—were my relatives on the McNally side, the family Charles McAllen had married into. McAllen married the one surviving girl in the McNally family, Mary Florence, who had been born right after my great-grandfather Peter.

In 1897, six of the John McNally children lived in or around Chokio: John, Jr. (Jack), James Henry (J. H.), Patrick Joseph (P. J.), Michael Peter (Mike), Peter H. (P. H.), and

Mary. Three of the children, William, Tom, and Joe, were living in Graceville, two towns to the west of Chokio. This is where Honora Reardon was from. Frank McNally had gone out to Wyoming and then on to California.

For much of the time that he ran the *Chokio Times*, McAllen used Willie McNally, William McNally's son, as a helper or "chief-push at the Times office," as reported in the paper. The first few issues of the paper are missing, but beginning with March 17, 1897, the History Center has all the issues.

The eight-page *Chokio Times* was published every Wednesday. International news was covered on the front page and a serial story, fashions for the women, plans for building houses, and national news filled the following pages. But the page that most interested me was the last page, the local news. Not only was the newspaper filled with information on my extended family, but Editor McAllen also had a good sense of humor and wasn't a bad writer, either.

The first issue I scanned was dated March 24, and I was pleased at how much information I obtained from it about the McNallys. I learned that "Mrs. P. J. McNally and Mrs. Edwin Lee were Morris visitors Monday." I found out that McAllen wasn't only the newspaper owner and editor but that he also ran the insurance agency in town for a company called German of Freeport. M. P. McNally placed an ad: "I have for sale several heavy draft horses, and one high grade short-horn bull, two years old; also wheat-house and wagon scales in Chokio."

The paper started right before the town was incorporated and reported on the process: "If we cannot have our town incorporated let us appoint a committee of the whole, and put in sidewalks the whole length of main street."

The final mention of the McNally family in that issue came in an article about a show put on by a lodge that McAllen belonged to: "The Woodman show St. Patrick's night was a marked success financially as well as socially. . . . The music furnished . . . by Mrs. P. J. McNally aided materially in making the play a success."

I never saw the introduction McAllen made to the community, but on August 18, 1897, the paper was six months old and he wrote:

> Six months ago yesterday the Times made its first appearance and though our success has not been quite what we expected, we nevertheless have had fairly good business and have grown steadily each week, and whether the paper has improved or not we leave our readers to judge. We intend, in the future to give the paper our undivided attention, and we will strive to make it a welcome visitor to every household in the locality, and a medium that will pay advertisers to patronize.

The *Chokio Times* often mentioned the weather, which should come as no surprise to Minnesotans. And the weather on this western border could be fierce. As spring came, its visit was noticed in the paper of March 31, 1897: "The lake in front of our office reached high-water mark Sunday. . . . The first meadow-lark of the season, sailed into town Friday alighted on a telegraph pole, and after proclaiming that spring had come, he stepped off on to a snow bank, registered and departed. . . . It is a trifle muddy." This last sentence can be nothing but an understatement, for there are no lakes close to Chokio's downtown area. The lake mentioned must have been newly formed of snow melt.

Because Chokio was a farming community, the weather was tied to agriculture. April 14, 1897: "Rather quiet town now, every body is seeding." June 2: "The frost Sunday night, done some damage to gardens." June 16: "Brown county, South Dakota, is infested with grasshoppers; some fields are reported entirely destroyed." "Rather surly looking clouds today; keep your eye on them." July 21: "Business is quiet in town this week, as farmers are busy haying." Then on September 15, a big storm hit:

> The worst wind storm of the season passed over this section Sunday afternoon at about 5 o'clock doing considerable damage to grain stacks, out buildings, barns, windmills, etc. The day had been oppressively hot with a sultry south wind until the hour above named, when the heavy dark cloud that had been forming in the northwest began to roll and twist in a manner that forboded a bad storm; suddenly the wind veared to the northwest and came down with a rush and roar that caused the people to look for places of safety. Tops were torn off grain and hay stack and sent whirling through the air, grain shocks were leveled in a great many places, and hayracks, machinery and lo[o]se buildings were tipped over. The worst damage so far is: Nels Husby, barn blown down and torn to pieces. J. M. Powers, windmill blown from the tower. P. H. McNally, granary blown off foundation, and a valuable dog which had went under the granary to escape the storm, crushed so badly that it had to be killed.

Weather reports in the newspaper today tend to predict what the weather will be, not tell what it has been. The *Chokio Times*'s constant quiet comments on the weather tickled me. December 22: "The shortest day of the year." January 26, 1898: "This is the last of January 1898; and if any old settler has ever seen a January that equaled the one just passing we would like to see him. We have had neither cold weather, wind, rain or snow: just nice quiet warm days, starry nights and such mornings that even editors get up early to see the mirage and hear the roosters crow." February 23, 1898: "The last two weeks have been rather on the winter order."

As the paper decreased in size and increased in announcements and advertisements, its comments on the weather became more infrequent but were still welcome to me. May 4, 1898: "Crop prospects are growing brighter every day. The rain of Saturday was just what was needed and grain and grass has taken a splendid start."

When I think of Chokio, I see the town as a gemstone in a setting, and I'm amazed at how the land holds this small group of buildings in its grip. As you drive into Chokio, the sign welcoming you to the town has the skyline in silhouette. Towering over this townscape are the grain elevators.

I had a teacher in college, an English professor, who told our class, "If you want to know what matters to a town, look at the tallest buildings." His theory certainly holds true for Chokio: grain and farming are the very reason for the town's existence. At the height of the town's prosperity, there were six elevators operating next to the railroad tracks.

Reading through the *Chokio Times,* I traced the development of what would become known as the Farmer's Elevator. On July 7, 1897, McAllen wrote:

> With the prospects for an abundant harvest in sight, would it not be a good plan for the farmers around Chokio to talk up a farmers elevator for Chokio. [C]o-operative elevators usually do not succeed well for the reason that the stock is transferable and the organizers are not careful enough in keeping sharks and shysters out of the company, who just as soon as business is started begin depressing the stock so they can buy a controlling interest from dissatisfied members, or refuse to stand their share of the expense thus throwing a too heavy load on the other stock holders. There is enough good responsible farmers around Chokio to form a company having plenty of means to erect and maintain a modern elevator at this place and that it would [be] a paying investment is beyond question.

In the September 29, 1897, issue, McAllen continued to encourage the formation of a co-operative elevator:

> We have heard it claimed that the price of wheat in Morris was from 3 to 5 cents higher than here and that Johnson was also paying more. This difference in the price is due to the fact that other towns have independent or farmers elevators, who compel the elevators to pay up, while here, "They will get the grain anyway." It is a good thing to call farmers attention to this difference in price in towns where there is independent houses and where there is none. A co-operative elevator, not only helps the stock-holders but it helps every farmer in the vicinity who has a bushel of grain to sell.

Then, the following spring, he wrote:

> Farmer's Elevator
> A meeting is Called for Saturday May
> 7th at 2 p.m. The Best Farmers Are Interested.

> Elswhere in to-day's paper is notice of a call, issued by a committee of our most prominent farmers, for a meeting to be held in this village. . . . The purpose of the meeting is to get the views of all who are interested regarding the question of building a farmer's elevator in Chokio. This is a question that should interest every man having a bushel of wheat to sell and he should make an effort to be present and express himself. A rightly conducted, farmers elevator will save to its owners from 2 to 4 cents on every bushel of wheat they have to market and this with an average yield will mean to the farmers of Chokio and vicinity many thousand dollars; and the farmers are not the only ones benifited the merchant and shop keeper derives an equal or greater profit than does any one farmer, and they should all lend their influence to help the matter along.

The meeting was a success, the paper reported:

> Farmer's Elevator.
> A assured thing.
> About 40 solid farmers met last Saturday in McNally Bros.,

warehouse and decided unanomously in favor of erecting a farmers elevator here this summer. There was not one dissenting voice. Every man present seemed to think that he had paid toll to the elevator companies long enough.

At this meeting M. P. McNally was voted president, and C. E. McAllen clerk. John McNally was appointed to a committee of five selected to look into how other farmers' elevators were run. The next meeting went well. The members set up their articles of incorporation, with capital stock of $3,000, divided into 250 shares at $20 apiece. No member could own more than three shares at a time. To own a share, one's principal business had to be farming. P. H. McNally and M. P. McNally each bought one and John, Jr., bought two.

On August 10, the *Chokio Times* described the grain elevator: "The building is to have a capacity of 20,000 bushel, to rest on a stone foundation and to be provided with dump and weighing-out scales." And on August 31, the newspaper reported that the elevator would be ready to receive grain on or before September 10 of that year.

Today, Chokio has four grain elevators operating next to the railroad tracks. They are all owned by the Chokio Equity Exchange, which started business in 1913 and slowly bought out the other elevator businesses.

❦

Charles McAllen often used the *Chokio Times* to report on news of particular interest to the Irish community. In the September 15, 1897, issue, he remarked:

Ireland is threatened with a terrible famine the coming winter as the wet weather has ruined the potato crop and the oat crop has been beaten into the ground by heavy rain and wind.

To add to the distress of these poor, down-trodden people, the landlords are pressing for their rent, and the saving tenant who may have a small amount in the saving bank, must draw it out and pay the rent on land from which he will get no crop, while himself and family must face the winter with a full knowledge that before spring gaunt starvation may stare them in the face.

On an odd note, in the February 15, 1898, issue, he told a joke of a visitor to Minneapolis:

An exchange says that an Irishman went into an eating house in Minneapolis and asked for a "square meal." The waiter first brought him a bowl of soup which Pat drank with a relish. She then brougt in celery which went the way of the soup. She then brought a fine lobster. He looked at the lobster a minute and then replied: "Madam," he said, "Oive drank you dishwater and ate your boquet but Oill be dom'd if oill ate that bug."

In both these stories, I could feel McAllen's remove. He was a second-generation Irish American who wasn't living off the land but rather off his wits. While he may have felt compassion for the country his parents left behind, he was no longer one of the "poor, down-trodden people," just as he was not the Irishman who didn't know a lobster from a bug. He was a newspaperman who could make a joke about the situation.

In a later issue, when countering an attack from the *Morris Sun,* McAllen drew on his Irish heritage:

This reminds us of the Irishman who, with a fork on his shoulder, was passing a house when a meddlesome dog rushed out and savagely attackted him; whereupon Patrick, in self defense, pinned the brute to the ground with his fork. The owner of the dog then came upon the scene and in a threatening manner asked; "why did you stab my dog?"— "Because he was trying to bite me." "Why didn't you come at him with the other end of the fork!" "why,["] says Pat, "didn't he come at me with his other end."

What I scoured the newspaper for was news of the McNally family, particularly the P. H. McNally family, but in reading the paper so intensely I discovered other tidbits. I was surprised to discover that women were never mentioned by their first names. Once they married, they assumed their husband's name, so Honora was always referred to as Mrs. P. H. McNally or as Peter McNally's wife. Children were only written about when they were born or when they died. This meant I couldn't hope to find any specific mention of three-year-old Mae McNally. But in noticing what her parents did, I could guess how her days were filled.

At the time the *Chokio Times* started up, the Peter McNally family was living out on the farm southeast of town. Editor McAllen was good friends with Peter and mentioned him often in the paper.

On March 31, 1897: "P. H. McNally, was a business visitor to Morris on Saturday."

On June 16:

P. H. McNally and family, W. J. McNally and family of Graceville, Ye Editor and family and Willie Bill, spent Friday and Saturday of last week at Mcgaughy's Park on Bigstone Lake.

This is one of the finest parks on the lake, and those who go there can be assured of courteous treatment and a pleasant time. The prices for stabling, tents, boats, bait etc., are very reasonable and Mr. McGoughy and his pleasant wife, assisted by the gentlemen in charge of the boats, will leave nothing undone to make your stay at the [p]ark one to be remembered with pleasure.

July 7:

The always glorious Fourth passed off pleasantly in Chokio and vicinity. . . . Eight children and twenty grandchildren gathered at Grand-Pa McNally's commodious home in South Baker and spent the national holiday in the shady grove where a splendid dinner, with side dishes, glasses and firecrackers galore composed the greater part of the programme for an afternoons enjoyment and rest.

September 8: "A large number of sportsmen went out to Pete McNally's duck pond Sunday afternoon, of course they had a good time, but you mustn't [be too] inquisitive regarding the number of birds brought in."

September 29: "P. H. McNally lost four hogs last week by a disease closely resembling hog cholera."

November 24: "The Editor and regiment will join P. H. McNally's full company in an attack on the 'Turks,' on the blue-grass farm to-morrow." Farther down on the page, a notice read: "Lost. A large pocket book containing about $20, somewhere between Pete's McNally's place and Chokio, or in Chokio. Finder will please return the same to this office and receive reward of $5.00."

Then, sadly, in the January 26, 1898, issue, I read the obituary of Peter and Honora McNally's third child:

Died.

Mr. and Mrs. P. H. McNally were called upon last Wednesday to mourn the loss of their fifteen months old son Urban. The little fellow was taken seriously ill Sunday and a physician sent for, who pronounced his ailment obstruction of the bowels. The case was of such a nature that medicine failed to help the little one and as a last resort, an operation was performed, which of itsself was successful, but the patient, already weak from pain, was unable to rally and he passed away shortly after undergoing the operation. Little Urban was a bright and loveable child and his loss is keenly felt by his doting parents, who have the sincere sympathy of the whole community in their sorrow. The funeral took place Friday morning; the remains being laid to rest in the new Catholic cemetery.

Only an empty cradle,
The parent's hearts forlorn
Sighing in mournful measure
The flight of their stolen treasure
Dead, in his childhoods morn.

A form in the twilight kneeling
Down by the empty nest,
A mothers heart-strings throbbing
In broken whispers sobbing
"Dear Lord, Thou knoweth best."

This obituary was the longest to appear in the *Chokio Times* and in many ways the most heartfelt. It was obvious that the two families were close and that McAllen was a loving uncle to Urban. I've wondered if the poem were a well-known lyric of the time, but I've concluded it was probably written by McAllen to express the sorrow he felt and the grief he saw in Honora McNally, who was already four months pregnant with her next child.

On March 16, 1898: "While on his way to town Thursday morning, P. H. McNally received a severe fall by the horse he was riding falling on the frozen ground with his rider; as a consequence of which Pete is nursing a bruised wrist that will inconvenience him for some time."

On June 15, 1898, some good news: "The home of Mr. and Mrs. P. H. McNally was made glad Thursday evening by the arrival of a bouncing baby girl. The Times extends hearty congratulations." This new arrival was Edna Delphine McNally.

⏤❀⏤

From reading all the *Chokio Times'* news of the Peter McNally family, I put together a good composite view of their life out on the western prairies of Minnesota. The paper caught a sense of excitement about what the settlers were accomplishing. Maybe much of this came from Charles McAllen, but I think it was also the era. The American-born children of the Irish immigrants were growing up. They were grabbing hold of their lives and they were full of energy. They were building houses and barns and banks, buying land and selling crops and farm equipment and insurance; they were having children and voting for the president of the United States.

The settlers worked hard, making use of all that was around them. To entertain themselves, they hunted and fished and played ball games. They danced and sang at each other's houses. They supported their schools and had debates and plays to keep their minds alert. They celebrated the Fourth of July. Judging from the amount of space Independence Day received in the paper, it was a much bigger occasion than Christmas. Towns vied with each other for the best celebrations. Children were included in much that the parents did. There were few babysitters except for the older children in the family.

They were proud of their children. They had their pictures taken when the children were small. I have pictures of Hugh, Mae, and Urban taken when they were infants. The photographs were all obviously taken the same day, but the children sat for their portraits separately. Hugh appeared to be almost five, Mae close to four, and Urban about one and a half. Hugh was dressed in a little tweed suit with knickers and a big white bow tied under his chin. His hands were in his pockets and he stared right at the camera, a look of apprehension on his small face, his ears sticking out from under his short haircut.

Urban was dressed in a white frilly frock and was seated in an elaborate wicker chair. He held a small toy in his hand and his face was blurred; he must not have sat still. He did not survive the year.

Mae looked the most at ease in a lovely white dress with lace around the collar. She did not look at the camera but slightly to the side, and she had a dreamy look on her face.

I can recognize her as my grandmother. I don't know how this is possible, but I can tell it's Mae by her eyes. There is something in her clear gaze that I find familiar. Mae always had a steady look.

❧

By the end of reading the one-year-and-nine-month run of the *Chokio Times,* I had settled into quite an easy routine of skimming the papers. But I received a jolt as I perused the May 11, 1898, issue. By this time, I was very good at picking out the names that meant something to me. I could scan a page quickly and pick out any mention of a McNally, then read to see if it was worth noting. But suddenly a very different name caught my eye. The announcement read: "Miss Mary Logue, visited in town Saturday."

I felt as if I had been caught doing something I wasn't supposed to. How did they know that I had been visiting? Like a writer appearing in her own novel or Alfred Hitchcock popping up in his own movies, seeing my own name in a hundred-year-old paper hit me strongly. I have known only one other Mary Logue in my life, and she is alive now. I discovered that a Mary Logue lived with her parents and siblings in Darnen Township, near Morris, in 1898. She was twenty-seven years old and had been teaching school for three years. At her age, I had worked in the Writers-in-the-Schools program for several years. She might well have been related to me, for there are few Logues, even in Ireland. However, her parents immigrated from Canada and my Logue relatives came up from Ohio.

❧

Charles McAllen had many other pots on the stove. After running the *Chokio Times* for a little over a year and a half, he decided to put it up for sale. The last issue of the newspaper came out on September 7, 1898. On the front page, McAllen explained the new arrangement:

> With this issue the present editor of The Times, retires from editorial control of the paper to be succeeded by Mr. J. A. Campbell of Morris, who has purchased The Times outfit and will take possession to-day. Hereafter the mechanical work of getting out the paper will be done in Morris but this will in no way effect the Chokio news as more space will be occupied in the new paper, in the interests of Chokio and vicinity than was the case under the old plan.

McAllen was optimistic about how Chokio news would be treated in this new paper. Many changes came with the new owner. The *Chokio Times* was the only Democratic paper in the county; Campbell's paper, the *Republican Times,* was just what the name claimed—staunchly Republican. For nearly a year, part of a page was devoted to Chokio news, but this dwindled out in August 1899.

I found a few tidbits about the McNallys in the *Republican Times.* On September 21, 1898: "P. H. McNally is letting his whiskers grow so he will look savage when he goes collecting for the machine firm of which he is a member."

The paper mentioned when the John McNally, Sr., family went to Morris to have their family picture taken on September 25, 1898. Then on October 19: "Mr. and Mrs. John McNally Sr. intend to leave their farm in south Baker, and take up their residence in Chokio. May they find the rest and contentment that they have richly earned in their new home."

Not too long afterward, the Peter McNally family followed suit as was reported on January 11, 1899: "Pete McNally has purchased John Hagen's house and will move into it with family as soon as possible." Then on March 15: "Pete McNally and family removed to town Tuesday." Pete and

Honora had decided to move to town so that their children could go to school there. When my grandmother was close to five, she left the farm, never to return, and moved into Chokio with her family.

⚮

What kind of town was Mae moving into? An article published in 1897 in the *Morris Tribune* gave a good picture of Chokio and the enthusiasm of the second-generation immigrants for the towns they were founding. The piece was filled with superlatives claiming Chokio was "a thriving little village that promises to outstrip her sister burgs," and that the land around Chokio was "of a rich dark loam, which is of inexhaustible fertility and excels anything in the state for general farming and stock raising. The formation of the soil is peculiar, inasmuch as it retains moisture and will withstand extreme drouth." These last words proved not to be true in the 1930s.

With a population of about 150 inhabitants, Chokio had twenty-eight "places of business, all in thriving and prosperous condition." Included in the list of businesses were three general stores, two blacksmith shops, two restaurants, two hotels, two churches, and two saloons. With a population less than one-third the size of Chokio in 1990, the town and surrounding countryside easily supported five times as many businesses.

⚮

After the incredible resilience and luck of the John McNally family—eleven children raised safely to adulthood, both parents dying in old age—Peter and Honora McNally had comparatively hard times. Four of their nine children died before they were ten. In 1916, Honora McNally died suddenly at the age of forty-four. My aunt Pat claimed that

Honora died of a heart attack, but her death record stated that the death was caused by "acute articulate Rheumatism." I wonder if a broken heart didn't enter into it all—the loss of four children taking its toll on her.

Grandma Carrie McNally, who married Mae's first cousin Ray, recalled Honora, or "Nan," as she was called, as a nice, stout woman who let Pete, her husband, have his way. Pete was a nasty old bugger—I'm quoting her here—and he had a mean Irish temper. Possibly the death of his four children turned him bitter.

The *Morris Tribune* carried an article on Honora's death:

Mrs. McNally Dies at Evening Meal
Well Known and Highly Respected
Chokio Woman Called Suddenly at Her Home

One of the saddest deaths in the county for some time occurred at Chokio last Saturday evening when Mrs. P. H. McNally suddenly expired after eating a light supper with members of her family. She was one of the well known, popular and highly respected women of the west end of the county and her death has cast a pall over the community.

The funeral was held Tuesday morning at 10:30 from the Chokio Catholic church with a sermon by Rev. Hengarten at the grave. A large concourse of friends gathered to pay their last respects, and the floral tributes were many and very beautiful. Miss Katherine Griffith, a life-long friend and a bridesmaid at the wedding of the deceased, were among those from his city who attended the funeral. During the funeral Chokio stores were closed.

. . . Besides the husband, four daughters and one son survive. They are Hugh, May, Edna, Irene and Margaret.

A picture of the four remaining girls was probably taken around 1918. They are all lying on their stomachs on the grass, facing the camera, their legs kicked up and crossed behind them, arms under their chins and folded the same way in front of them. It's a very posed picture. They all have

*The McNally sisters, about 1918, Chokio. Left to right:
Marguerite, Edna, Irene, and Mae*

long hair pulled back from their faces. They're smiling and
lined up in a row. I have no picture of Hugh McNally when
he was older.

⟿

Hugh, the oldest child, graduated from high school in
Chokio in 1910 and went on to the University of Minnesota.
He served in the officers' training corps during the First
World War. After the war, he moved out to Montana and settled in Miles City. He married Catherine Mary Hogl and they
had four children. He returned to Chokio at least once, when
Mae's husband died in 1926. He moved again, to Portland,
Oregon, where he worked as a structural engineer for the
Milwaukee Road. He died in 1937 of a heart attack at the age
of forty-three years—nearly the same age his mother died—
and his children had never even visited Chokio. Mae's daughter, my aunt Pat, doesn't remember ever meeting him,
although she named her first son for him.

After Mae came Edna. She went to school at St. Mary's Academy but didn't graduate. She then tried to go into nursing, but she was unable to complete the course. She returned home to care for her complaining father. In 1922, when she was twenty-four, she married Albert Reichmuth, who was several years younger than she but who had a job at the bank. She put on airs that are mentioned to this day. Albert, by all accounts, was a nice, quiet man who enjoyed living in Chokio.

According to Edna's daughter Donna Reichmuth, Edna admired Mae a great deal but was also jealous of her, possibly because Mae finished school and she didn't. Edna was very conscious of wanting to be a "lace-curtain Irish and not a shanty Irish." After Mae married and left Chokio, Edna assumed responsibility for her younger sisters. She continued to take care of Irene all her life.

When Irene was born on March 7, 1901, her twin sister was stillborn. Irene weighed two-and-a-half pounds at birth. As she grew up, she developed problems. At age fourteen, she was reported to have been extremely nervous and irritable. People were cautious of her. She attended school up to the eighth grade. Later, she was trained in "beauty culture" at a school in the Twin Cities. But as Grandma Carrie said of her, "she would go dancing in the park, talking to the trees." She was a handsome girl with beautiful thick brown hair.

Before 1925, according to the family, Irene had been "peculiar at times for several years." Several people recalled her being violent. My aunt Pat remembers a story about the time that Irene got really angry and threw an iron at Marguerite.

I had never heard of my great-aunt Irene before I started working on this book. But as I asked my relatives about her, it didn't appear that she was a secret, merely that she had been forgotten. She was alive until I was fourteen years old, yet I never met her, never heard any mention of her, or knew of her funeral. My mother must surely have gone to it.

At age twenty-four, she had an "attack"—a nervous breakdown. From her medical files, I read about this breakdown, the symptoms of which were that she "Did not sleep nor eat and was fearful of being hurt. Sudden. Increasing. Desire to run away. Fits of temper." She was voluntarily committed to Rochester State Hospital in April 1925. Then she was released and went home to stay with her father and worked at a beauty shop in Graceville. In October of that same year, she was again committed, this time to Fergus Falls State Hospital.

After I found out that Irene existed, I called Fergus Falls Regional Treatment Center, as it is now known, and asked for any records they might have on her. The women at the records office were very helpful. They wrote back and told me that "due to voluminous size of this chart, information sent to you was basic information." They also let me know that the chart would be destroyed in 1997 but that it could be sent to me if I wanted it. I assured them I did.

The basic information I was sent was a twenty-page, double-sided, single-spaced series of notes from her lifetime in the hospital. I sat right down and read them through. When I was done, I read them again. This story of a nervous breakdown—attack, insanity, disorder, dementia praecox, paranoid type, manic-depression, mental illness, what have you—was fascinating and quite unnerving. How did it happen to her? Why was she treated the way she was? How could they have treated her otherwise? How would she have been handled today? Would she have been given Prozac? There are no answers to these questions, but I felt the need to ask them.

On October 5, 1925, her file began with her commitment to Fergus Falls. The first entry reads:

> This young woman's mind is very active. She is quick of comprehension; pays attention to what is said to her; she is also a ready talker. She says that she was in Rochester for a couple of months and that she did not like it there, that they did not do anything for their patients, etc. She says there was a conspiracy on foot between the nurses and the woman physician; that things did not go the way they should and the way they treated the insane was inhuman, etc.
>
> This girl minimizes every statement made in the commitment. She says that she slept good at home; that she did not eat because she had a pain in her side; that she always lunched in the forenoon and afternoon and ate between times which made up for her failure to eat at meal time. She certainly looks well nourished and has not suffered greatly from lack of food. She denies that she was afraid of being harmed. Claims that she is afraid of nothing and that she just goes to the other extreme. She tells us that when she worked in the beauty parlor in Graceville she had a funny and unpleasant sensation when she was in the room alone, but that she does not know what caused it.

Information was also included from Rochester State Hospital, telling that two of the patient's sisters had had nervous breakdowns—one while in high school, the other after a baby was born. Mae had had four children by 1925, and Edna had had two, so either of them could have been one of the sisters Irene described.

Through the end of 1925, Irene was quite unstable. She became delusional and was transferred to a more secure ward. But in 1926, she began to improve. By the end of March, she was paroled to her father and allowed to return to Chokio. In November 1926, she was officially discharged by the state. She earned a living as a traveling saleslady for Kranks Company, selling cosmetics.

The first symptoms of her next attack started in July 1929. The medical file described them: "Melancholia. Hallucinations. Irritable and threatening bodily harm to others if crossed."

She was recommitted to Fergus Falls in January 1930. The file notes read: "She is a woman twenty-nine years of age of average frame and well nourished. Her expression is stubborn. . . . She is oriented correctly for time and place, is clear and talks readily. She is silly and very changeable and temperamental."

Then Irene turned violent. By August 1931, she was attacking the nurses and had to be kept in restraints. Her weight dropped from 132 to 118 pounds in 1932. Her moods varied widely; sometimes she was allowed to work and to stay in a more congenial ward, and sometimes she was very agitated and had to be kept in restraints.

By April 1934, her condition was very serious:

> This patient has increasing frequent disturbed periods lasting two or three months. In the interval she is pleasant, rational and quiet, working on the ward and at the Industrial. She is at present going through a manic attack and is boisterous, abusive, sometimes violent and very persecuted. She constantly accuses the nurses of starving her to death and giving her filthy spoiled food, but actually she eats very well. Has been in jacket much of the time the past two months.

Irene was then transferred to Anoka State Asylum. Seven years later, she returned to Fergus Falls for an operation on her fibroid tumors. By this time, she was forty years old. The admission notes let me hear her:

> States, "If I can eat and sleep, I am all right." Remarked that she had gained eight pounds since she had been here. She is illogical at times in her reasoning and shows poor judgement. She stated that she started school at the age of two and was in high school at the age of eleven and that the age

we had on our records was wrong because she was considerably younger. She states, "The operation is for nothing, but I would rather pay for it." "I have had an operation before and there was no incision, if there is no incision it heals faster." "I have gone through the Mayo Clinic at Rochester and I was all right then." One doctor, she says, told her she was the most perfect person physically he had ever seen.

Irene was heavily sedated, given Betaplexin, Creamelin tablets, thiamin chloride, and sodium luminol. Notes from June 20, 1941, indicated: "She is quite cooperative as to nursing care at present when she is kept in restraint, but becomes resistive when she is taken out. The type of restraint used is camisole and foot cuffs."

Her operation was put off because she had come down with a fever. Irene then slipped into a bad state. The next note was from October 1941:

Weight 118 pounds. Patient is in cuffs, is oriented in three spheres, has no insight, does no work, has poor appetite and is occasionally tube fed, she sleeps poorly, is untidy, talkative, destructive, combative, resistant, agitated, changeable, preoccupied, suspicious, incontinent, and vulgar.

By January 1942, she weighed only 104 pounds. Her mood and weight swung up and down for the next six years. Finally, in 1948, she had her surgery to remove the tumors. In 1950, she received a letter from her sister Edna, who was now the wife of the executive vice president of the Chokio State Bank. The scene was described in the notes:

A hypomanic, plump and steelgray-haird lady with face peppered with goose-pimples and blackheads, ruddy complexion, approaches the Ward Physician waving the letter from Mrs. A. J. Reichmuth . . . in his face, and insisted that her supposed father, a Dr. John McNally and a supposed Uncle, a lawyer, Mr. John McNally, be written to for the purpose of getting the patient out of here. She claims to be a "graduate" of a Beauty Parlour School, and to be a licensed operator, having had a very successful business of her own in Minneapolis in years gone by. There "never was any good reason why she was placed here." Dr. Akester knows her well and says she is a fabricator. No improvement.

In 1950, the staff started administering electric shock treatment (EST) to Irene. For a while, it was helpful. By April 1951, she had undergone sixty-four treatments. At that point, Irene was considered for a lobotomy. By September 1951, the doctors reported that twice-weekly EST was "no longer sufficient to control her overactivity, combativeness, and destructiveness." She was put on phenobarbital and sodium luminol for sedation, plus small doses of hyocine.

Irene was given a bilateral frontal lobotomy on May 1, 1952, fifteen days after I was born.

A month later, on June 17, 1952, Irene wrote to her sister, my grandmother Mae:

> My life has been very miserable. The weather now is very nice. It would not take any of you very long to drive over here and get me. My physical health would improve away from here. I have not done anything to cause you misery. I would be outdoors more and get better food. I hope your family are all very (P.S. turn paper) healthy. You would have to try and live here a while to know my attitude.
>
> Have you heard from Marguerite and Hugh. [They had both died—Hugh in 1937 and Marguerite in 1947.] They used to try and get along with me sometimes. Maudie would like to have me with her. We get along fine together. If I wrote Hugh he would come and get me. How is he? Hope to see you very soon. Greet my relatives and friends. I suppose your children have grown so I should hardly know them. [Four of Mae's children had already married and one had died.] I hope Edna is very well. I received a nice letter from her. P.S. I certainly would be happy to see some of you. I have quite a crowd of trailers you know what they are like.

After her surgery, Irene seemed better. The medical notes reported that only once or twice a month would she get "sarcastic." In 1953, the psychologist reported on her family: "Her relatives do not pay much attention to her. . . . It is felt that she probably deliberately frightens her sisters when they visit by acting much 'nuttier' than she really is. It is almost as if she is playing a joke on her relatives and gets big kick out of it."

I have a photograph of Irene that I think is from around this time. It is a kind of mug shot, with Irene's name printed under her face. Her hair is shoulder length and side waved, turning gray, but quite nice looking. She is wearing a polka-dot dress and looking just to the side of the camera. Her smile is pulled in, as if she is resisting it.

Irene worked in the sewing room and dining room of the state hospital for the next few years. In 1954, her doctors considered letting her out but didn't feel she was ready. In 1958, a doctor reported: "She seems to have a little difficulty walking. Perhaps she has had a cerebral accident of some kind. At the present time she is not as difficult as she used to be. Patient is psychotic but today is fairly amicable."

Irene McNally at the Fergus Falls State Hospital, n.d.

In March 1964, she was re-evaluated: "This patient came in readily, was very verbal, and states her health is good but she is getting to be crippled. She presents a picture of a typical lobotomized patient. She talks constantly all day long, does nothing on the ward and does just as she pleases. She cares for herself and is fairly neat. She enjoys men's company more than women." Irene was being given thorazine, phenobarbital, and Artane.

I have a photograph of her dated 1964. This time her name was hand-printed under her mug shot. She is slumped crooked, wearing a paisley cotton dress with her bra strap showing. Her hair is cut to a practical ear-length and has turned gray. She looks as if she is drunk or quite drugged. Her eyes are shut and she's wearing a goofy, contemptuous smile on her face.

In early 1967, the asylum staff seriously considered discharging her forty-two years after she was first committed. One of her doctors wrote:

> It is noted that this patient is now better. She does some mopping. She used to work in the bakery but ate too much

Irene McNally at the Fergus Falls State Hospital, 1964

there. She has been on a diet here and is losing weight. It was noted that the patient was rather mean for awhile in the past and has disturbed periods. Lately she has been much better. She does go off ward to the store. She makes her bed and others' and takes fairly good care of herself. It was noted that she hit Harold Nelson once and occasionally will strike another patient. In the past she was angry because she had no pension. Her plans have always been unrealistic, wanting to go out into the cosmetics business. The patient is from Chokio and has a brother there and her hope right now is for a steady job and in this she is rather unrealistic, not recognizing that her age is very definitely against her. It was interesting to note she gave the meaning of Chokio, stating it was named after an Indian name meaning "halfway" because it is halfway between Morris and Graceville. She mentioned that she has a sister in New York, a sister in Chokio and there was an older sister who was killed in an auto accident. She claims that her real father was an opera singer and an outlaw and needed to be locked up and that she was raised by foster parents. She was married at the age of 16 and is sort of separated. She denies that she is divorced, says she has two grown children who would be 48 and 50 now and she doesn't know where they are. She claims her husband was a doctor. When asked if she wanted to go to a rest home or might be interested in it, she says "No, I want to be at large." This patient has a tendency to kid you and pull your leg with the things she does say so it is a little difficult to tell the difference between what is the truth, what is kidding and what is delusional with this patient. It was felt that we should take her with us when we go out to see nursing homes so that she can get some idea of what they are like. She obviously has no idea what a nursing home is. Everyone commented today that she is as good now or better than she has ever been and discharge planning would be realistic.

Irene McNally, born at the turn of the century, died on October 14, 1967. She was discharged on this date. She died of shock from an infarction of the right lung, caused by an embolus of the right pulmonary artery. She was sent to the Olson Funeral Home in Morris, Minnesota. Joanie McNally remembered helping with the funeral at the church in Chokio. The only child from the Peter and Honora McNally family now left alive was Edna.

After reading the one letter written by Irene to Mae, I wondered if there were more correspondence that had not been sent to me. I called up the Fergus Falls Treatment Center again and asked if they could check Irene's file for me. The woman in the records office told me that in looking over the file, she had in fact found many more letters. I asked her to send them to me. Hanging up the phone, I was so excited I could hardly stand it. When I started this project, I had hoped to come across a packet of letters written by Mae to someone. But I quickly realized that almost everyone Mae knew lived in Chokio; why would she need to bother to write? Plus, no one in the family seemed to keep old letters.

Now there was a chance that I might get my wish. Possibly Mae had written regularly to Irene about her life and I would get to hear her describe it in her own words.

Two days later, a package arrived from Fergus Falls. I opened it with trembling fingers, then sat and stared at what I had been sent: photocopies of letter after letter from Edna Reichmuth to the superintendent of Fergus Falls, Dr. William L. Patterson, accompanied by money—three- to five-dollar checks—and asking how Irene was: "Dear Doctor, would you please advise me as to the condition of my sister. . . ." and short replies from him, quoting the notes from Irene's file. I was sorely disappointed.

But tucked into the middle of this huge stack of copies

were three letters from Irene that I read with interest. The first two were from March 1946 and were responses to job advertisements in the paper:

Dear, Mr Thurston:
   I read your ad in the Mpls Sun[day] paper. I have always done housework and know I am very good at it I am a very good cook. I understand all the phases of house keeping and like to do housework. I would like to hear from you as to salary and what will be expected of me. I would prefer to work in St Paul to here. I am employed at present but would go to St Paul.
   Sincerely, Irene E McNally
   Fergus Falls Minn
   Box 157.

Style Shop Browns Valley Minn
Dear, Madam:
   In regard to your ad in Mpls paper, I am a graduate in Beauty Culture, I have a teachers diploma and a managers liscence. I have owned and managed my own beauty shop and have been very successful. I am employed in a beauty shop at present but think I would prefer to work in Browns Valley. I would like to hear from you in regard to this position as to salary or commission and what would be expected of me. I would appreciate hearing from you at your earliest convenience.
   Sincerely,
   Irene E. McNally

I have to assume that because these letters were still in her file they had never been mailed or that they somehow had been confiscated. What strikes me most about them is how remarkably clear Irene seemed. She spelled most of the words correctly; she seemed to know the form for such letters; she managed not to mention where she was presently living. The hope contained in them is heartbreaking. What is worst to me is that they might simply have been seen as more evidence of Irene's inability to accept the reality of her situation—in other words, as more evidence of her insanity.

Irene's third letter was written in June 1946 to a doctor about her need for a gynecological operation, but again, it shows Irene's desire to leave the treatment center.

Dr. Thompson:
Dear, Dr. Thompson:

I am in need of a major operation as I am losing my insides. It will require surgery to put them back where they be long so that it is permanent. I also have two large tumors that should be removed. To delay only makes those conditions worse. I have a very good Dr. in St Paul who would know about what should be done all I have been released from this hospital previous. I would like to have a parole so I can get outdoors this nice weather. They need some one to work in employes dining room. Regina told to ask the Dr for a work card. It is a crime for me to spend any time here when I should be out enjoying my life. It won't belong before the Summer will be gone. Dr Wm. J. McNally of Mpls is also related to me. He could take care of me. Will appreciate hearing from you in . . . regard to this also to get work card and Parole. Thanking you for same I am

Sincerely
Irene E. McNally

I could find no record of the Dr. William J. McNally that Irene wrote about. She had an uncle named William J. McNally, but he was a teacher in Graceville. His son, William, Jr., was the boy who worked for Charles McAllen at the *Chokio Times*. The son would have been seven years older than Irene, but she must have known him well because he spent so much time in Chokio. Rather than becoming a doctor, however, he worked for the railroad and the power company. Irene seemed to be fabricating in this last letter. Her language was much more scrambled, but I have to agree that she should have been out enjoying her life.

Wanting a professional appraisal of the information I had received about Irene, I contacted Dr. William N. Friedrich, a consultant and professor of psychology at the Mayo Clinic and Medical School. After talking with him, I sent him Irene's medical records plus a sketch of her family history. I received back from him a three-page letter with his reactions to her case. Psychotherapy, he wrote, had changed in some ways and not in others—both lobotomies and EST are making comebacks.

What interested me most in his letter was his take on Irene's family. He began, "The early onset plus the history of psychological problems in siblings all would support some significant, family based problems." He explained this further on in his letter:

> Families in which mental illness is present in more than one person are frequently "centrifugal" families. These are families that are characterized by people being distant from each other or leaving the core of the family. Relationships are difficult among family members and are not cultivated the way they might be in families that are "centripetal". It is likely that Irene both bothered her siblings and they bothered her, or at least her parents did. It seems as if she and Olive [Marguerite] took similar tacks with one dying of alcoholism and the other one dying in an institution. But then you have an aunt Edna who married a banker and appears to have been successful. A very checkered family indeed. Mae and Edna are older than either Irene and Olive. You wonder almost if Honora didn't run out of steam, and the last several children were emotionally deprived and left more vulnerable to some of the tyranny of Peter. The fact that Irene's problems started at the age of 14, right around the time her mother died, would speak to how her mother's death had a lasting impact on her.

Dr. Friedrich commented on what he thought was wrong with Irene. One word from his analysis sticks with me:

I don't think manic depressive illness was your aunt's most appropriate diagnosis. She had paranoid features, hysterical conversion disorder features, manic features, and clearly depressive features. In addition, she was obnoxious, and at the time she was alive, society had even less use for obnoxious women than they do now. I really feel for her situation. Mental hospitals, even [in] the thirties and forties were used more often for women than men. The opposite was true of prisons and still is.

The word that I took from all this was *obnoxious*. The dictionary's first definition of this word was "exposed to danger." This certainly was true in Irene's case. I decided I liked the word; it had a good ring to it. I made a small pledge to Irene that in her honor, I would henceforth try to be more obnoxious.

⟝⟞

When I finished writing this section on Irene, I was drained. At first I had thought it would be easy to go through Irene's record, culling and presenting sections to show her life. But I could not stay unbiased: Irene was my great-aunt, and after reading about her, I wondered about the mental health of my family. Studies show that manic-depression runs in families, often concurrently with alcoholism; I have a sister who died of alcoholism and so did my grandmother Mae. Many relatives on my mother's side of the family have been known to drink too much.

I continued to puzzle—who were the two sisters who had nervous breakdowns? What about my mother's nervous breakdown when I was five, my sister Helen three, and our brother Jamie two? My mother was hospitalized and put on tranquilizers. My sister Robin told me later that Mom had said she also suffered from panic attacks.

Later, when I was in my teens, a neighbor woman had a nervous breakdown. My mother and a good friend sat at our kitchen counter, drinking iced tea and smoking cigarettes. The warm summer breeze floated in the window. I leaned at the corner of the counter, all ears about what I was hearing. My mother started to name all the women in the neighborhood who had suffered nervous breakdowns. Sometimes, she explained, "It just gets to be too much." She had not known that when she had kids her life would change so drastically. Little support from the hard-working husband. No outside life. "It breaks some women."

I could not distance myself from Irene and how she was treated by saying, *Oh, that was a long time ago, things have changed now, treatments are so much better,* because that's not true. Electric shock treatment has made a resurgence and is often used successfully for patients with depression. Lobotomies are still performed in the state of Minnesota; at least one doctor specializes in them.

Why did these things happen to Irene? Possibly her condition was simply encoded in her genes. But in looking at her life, three things stand out: one, she was a surviving twin; two, by the time she was ten years old, four of her siblings had died; and three, when she was fifteen, her mother died suddenly at the age of forty-four. Surely any one of these tragic occurrences could have triggered a breakdown in someone predisposed to it. What I continue to wonder is if she had had access to modern therapy and an easing of the drug regime, could she have lived a more normal, fulfilling life out in the world?

❧

Olive Marguerite became the baby of the family when her younger sister Ruth died in 1910. I heard a fair amount about my mother's aunt Marguerite while I was growing up, despite the fact that she had died five years before I was born. My mother admired her a great deal. Marguerite was sophisti-

Marguerite McNally, about 1945

cated, lovely, and dissolute, all seen as charming qualities to the young. Marguerite graduated from the Chokio schools in 1923 and taught in rural schools for several years. She and Irene went out to Albany, New York, and sold cosmetics for a while.

I would guess that my two large photographs of Marguerite were taken when she was near forty. They might even have been taken by my mother, who would have been close to twenty-five. My mother went out with a photographer for a while in her mid-twenties and kept a scrapbook of the many pictures she took in her own distinctive style—intimate portraits. Both of the pictures are close-up head shots of Marguerite. She is all dressed up in a short-sleeved sweater outfit decorated with pearls and angora embroidery and wears a string of large pearls around her neck. Looking world-weary, she is caught smoking and looking pensive. The smoke shoots from her mouth and mingles with the plume drifting up from her raised cigarette. Her dark brown hair is waved and just covers her ears. In the other picture, her head is tipped forward, and she peers off to the side of the camera with uplifted eyes. She is darkly somber and dramatic, with thin lips and freckles. Her family called her "Marty" and her husband called her "Mickey."

She married John "Jack" Mordica, who was quite a bit older than she, and they moved to Baltimore, Maryland, where he worked for Bethlehem Steel as a salesman. Eventually, she divorced him because of his binge drinking and moved back to Minneapolis. For the last nine years of her life, she was a circulation manager for the International Circulation Company, which had its headquarters in Minneapolis.

She died suddenly at the age of forty-one from cirrhosis of the liver. Although everyone was surprised that she died so young, the family knew she had a bad drinking problem. Mae and her daughters, Ruthmary and Pat, were visiting when Marguerite took sick. Pat was eight months pregnant with her first child, Hugh. The day before Marguerite went into the hospital, Aunt Pat did Marguerite's nails and hair, not realizing that anything much was wrong with her.

Marguerite's obituary says that she was taken suddenly ill at her home in Minneapolis and went to Northwestern Hospital, where she passed away after two days. My mother gave my youngest sister Dodie the middle name of Margaret. Marguerite McNally Mordica was buried in

Chokio's Catholic cemetery, next to her mother and father and other siblings.

───

What happened to Mae? Born in 1894, she grew up for the first four years of her life out on her father's farm south of Chokio. As the oldest daughter, she must have taken on many of the responsibilities of helping her mom run the house and watch the younger kids. For this reason, I would expect that the deaths of her siblings would have been especially hard on her. Moving into Chokio would have been wonderful for her—allowing her access to many more children to play with. She went to elementary school in Chokio and then was sent to St. Mary's Academy for her last four years of school, from age sixteen to twenty, graduating in 1914.

St. Mary's Academy was established in 1885 when four Sisters of the Order of St. Joseph of Carondelet arrived in Graceville, a town that Bishop Ireland had set up specifically for the Catholic Irish. They settled on a piece of property on the western edge of town and signed a contract with the federal government to educate the Dakota Indian girls from the Sisseton reservation. In 1888 Mother Cecelia Delaney was appointed as superioress of the Graceville Community and held this office for ten years. (When I saw her name, I realized whom my aunt Tead, born in Graceville, was named for. Her given name is Cecelia.)

In 1900, Archbishop Ireland procured the present-day site. The new church and school were built and named St. Mary's Academy. The school and its borders grew rapidly over the next decade with rooms added to buildings and new buildings erected. According to a sketch of the academy, "This boarding school was widely patronized by young ladies from the western part of the state and many elementary teachers were prepared here before graduation from normal school became a requirement. It is interesting to note that this was one of the very few places in the west where instruction could be obtained in music, painting, and other fine arts, in addition to the usual academic subjects." The school closed in 1959 when the costs of hiring competent teachers and renovating buildings in desperate need of repair became too high for the proposed budget.

When I first started this project and went out to Chokio, I called at the rectory and asked if I could look at the school records for my grandmother. I was told that they would look into it and get back to me. They didn't. Later, I called from Minneapolis and was told the same thing. Finally, when I was up in Chokio again, Kay Grossman and I decided to visit the church.

The pastor showed us his new computer and then said, yes, he thought there was a big box of old school records in the basement. We followed him down to a back room. He pointed to a box sitting on the basement floor but told me that he wasn't sure I could look at it because of confidentiality. I told him that Mary McNally, as she was known then, was my grandmother. If I didn't have a right to look at her records, then who did? So, with reluctance, he dug into the box. Finally he came to her final report card. It had all four years of her schooling marked on it. But he wouldn't allow me to look in the box and see if I could find anything more. The secretary made a photocopy of the report card and I went away, only slightly satisfied. The "Student's High School Record Card" lists her name as Mary J. McNally, her address as Chokio, and her parent as P. H. McNally.

During her first year of school, Mae received her lowest grades, but by her fourth year, they had risen considerably. I was surprised at the breadth of the courses she took—ranging from geometry to ancient history, Latin to German, physics to American literature.

In her final year, she received her best grades—two 87s in chemistry and American history, a 90 in English, a 92 in American literature, and a 94 in English history. After graduating from school, she worked in the post office with her father for six years.

The surviving pictures of Mae from this time show a happy, lovely, well-fed woman. There is a series of five pictures of her taken around 1918. In them she had long dark hair that she wore down in loose ringlets. In my favorite photograph, she was leaning back with her arms behind her

Mae, about 1918

"Private Turner," left, and Private Bill Kirwin sightseeing in Monte Carlo during World War I

head, her dress flapping in the wind, the trees dimpled behind her, and she looked as if she owned the world. In another one, she was dressed as a Red Cross nurse in a white outfit with a large white cap and veil, a red cross on her hat and on her chest. Her hands were clenched into fists and she wore white high-heel boots.

Sometime in 1915–16, Mae met James "Bill" William Kirwin, a short, handsome man with dark hair and blue eyes. Bill was from Morris and one year her senior. The oldest of eleven children, he was of Irish and German descent. His family had moved up from Iowa around 1905.

❦

After Mae and Bill met he went off to fight in World War I. They corresponded. My aunt Pat remembers reading a bundle of love letters that they wrote during the war. I tried to find these letters but never located them. According to the *Morris Tribune,* Bill "left Morris with what was known as the 'Cincinnati Bunch.' After three months training in Cincinnati, he went to France where he served as a truck driver."

Fortunately, I have a group of seven pictures from his war experience. One looks as if it was taken stateside—a group of twelve men against a barracks. I can't pick out my grandfather; possibly he took the picture. Then a photo that was taken on a ship, coming or going I can't be sure. There were six men in this photo, and my grandfather Bill was easy to pick out. He was sitting in uniform, his hat slightly askew on his head, a confident smile and one hand on top of the other on his knee.

The remaining five were taken in Europe. My grandfather wrote on the back of them: "Casino at Menton used by YMCA," "Statue in yard of the Prince of Monaco," "The bunch picture taken on promanade on the shore of the Mediteranean Sea," "Bunch taken in the yard in front of the Grand Hotel," and "Sightseeing in Monte-Carlo." In this last picture, Private Bill Kirwin was sitting behind his friend Private Turner and they were riding in a carriage pulled by a small donkey.

I can only hope the war was as fun for him as it appeared to be in these photographs, but I doubt it. Family history has it that he brought back from France a diamond for Mae and a dried-up human ear.

After his discharge from the service, Bill worked for the Standard Oil Company, driving a truck out of Morris. Then he tried his hand at farming in Pepperton Township for several years.

⟨⟩

Bill and Mae married on May 24, 1920, at St. Mary's Catholic Church in Chokio. The *Chokio Review* called Mae "one of Chokio's most charming and popular young ladies."

Irene McNally was Mae's maid of honor and George Kirwin, Bill's brother, was the best man.

I know their wedding took place on a lovely day because they took many pictures outside. Bill looked very proud in his dark double-breasted suit. He wore a white shirt with a white bow tie. Mae wore a lovely white lace dress with long sleeves, a white sash at the waist, and a head band with a full-length veil. Her two rings shone on her finger, peeking out below the lace sleeve. In one picture they stood close to each other, arms brushing. In the next picture, Bill turned toward Mae, the blur of his arm coming up to embrace her. Mae looked coyly at the camera, her hand to her mouth, her eyes smiling, and her rings glinting in the sun. Mae was twenty-six years old. She might have thought her real life had just begun.

Wedding day, May 24, 1920, Chokio. Left to right: James "Bill" Kirwin, the groom; Mae McNally Kirwin, the bride; Irene McNally, the maid of honor; George Kirwin, the best man.

In and Out
of the Depression
1920-1940

*Since no one's life can be really
known, since what is recorded or
remembered very much depends
on chance, as biographers and
readers of biography, we all choose
among the relics to form the life we
want to envision for our subject.*

Carolyn G. Heilbrun
"Dorothy L. Sayers: Biography between the Lines"

Overleaf: Mae, 1938

Out of all the days of Mae Kirwin's life, the one I have wondered about the most is February 16, 1926. She would have been thirty-one years old. Calvin Coolidge was the president and Theodore Christianson was the governor of Minnesota. The tremblings of the Depression were being felt on the edge of the prairies—the farmers had had a couple of rough years already. Farm prices had been on a steady decline since 1921. I imagine Mae waking up on that cold winter day in the small southern Minnesota town of Winnebago. It was Shrove Tuesday, the last day of festivity before the season of Lent begins.

Mae had four children to feed; the oldest was my mother Ruthmary, who was nearly five, and Mae was eight months pregnant with her fifth. She and her husband had run the Kirwin Cafe in town but then had sold it. Now her husband Bill was away, employed by the Interstate Power Company in Iowa. That day he was working in Swea City, about forty-two miles to the southwest. I can see her stirring around the kitchen on that cold morning, cooking something warm like oatmeal, when the phone rang, or more probably someone walked over to tell her the news. Her husband was dead.

Her hands, I can almost tell you what she did with her hands. One flew to rest on her swollen belly, protecting the new life she was carrying, and the other settled on the head of one of her youngsters. Maybe she looked at Jim, who at three was the second oldest. He already looked like his father. Her children were all she had left of her husband. They had not even been married six years. She was far from her own family and must have felt very alone. She probably cried, then tried to pull herself together for her children. She was all they had now. From what I know of Mae, she would have resolved to do what she needed to do to keep her children with her.

Throughout the day, she would learn more of his death. Bill hadn't felt well the day before, which was a Monday. He had left work early and gone back to his hotel. He went to sleep and on Tuesday morning his roommate couldn't wake him up. He was dead. Thirty-three years old. Dead of an acute heart attack, according to the coroner's report. The coroner, W. E. Laird, noted that a contributing factor to his death was a severe cold.

This heart condition would show up again and again in his immediate family when his younger brothers also died of heart attacks at relatively young ages—43, 52, 58, 63. Bill had already passed the condition on to his children—my mother would suffer her first heart attack at forty-two and her brother Jim would die at fifty-seven from a heart attack.

Bill Kirwin's death was reported in many of the small town newspapers around the Iowa-Minnesota border. The *Swea City Herald* mentioned it, as did the *Blue Earth Post.* In the *Winnebago City Press-News,* there appeared an obituary of this man who had lived in their community for several years.

> For some time Mr. Kirwin was engaged in the restaurant and confectionery business in Winnebago. After selling out his business he entered the employ of the electric company. He leaves a wife and four children, besides a large circle of friends to mourn his sudden and untimely death. Deceased was a member of the Catholic church, also of Winnebago Post No. 82 American Legion.

All the written reports I've read say the same thing: he died from heart failure. But there is a family myth about this death, one that I'm not sure I've completely figured out. I had always heard from my mother that her father Bill received an electric shock up on the power line that Monday—that he didn't feel good and, not too long after, his heart failed. My aunt Pat swears this is what Mae told the children. But nowhere in any of the written accounts of his death have I been able to find the slightest hint that there was any kind of electrical accident the day that Bill Kirwin died.

It's odd to grow up accepting something as a fact and then to do research that leaves me uncertain about the truth. I searched all of the newspapers that wrote about his death just to see if there was any mention of anything out of the ordinary. Admittedly, dying of heart failure at thirty-three is not usual, but I did find a clue that might explain this Kirwin family myth.

On the day that my grandfather died, an article appeared in the *Blue Earth Post* about a young man who had received a serious injury while working for a power company. His name was Ronald Weiler. He was an employee of a high-line repair crew and was working in Decorah, Iowa. What is amazing about this young man is that he had previously been in another power-line accident, had been seriously burned, and had lost an eye. According to the *Post,* the second accident was "caused by a misunderstanding of orders on the part of the man in charge of the power house at Decorah regarding cutting out certain voltage lines at certain hours."

Three other men were with Weiler, but they escaped without serious injury: "They tell that when young Weiler came into contact with the wire, his body resembled a large ball of fire, and how he escaped instant death is myraculous." Two of the other men were so upset by what had happened that they went home for a few days.

A week later, when the *Post* reported on Bill Kirwin's death, the fate of Ronald Weiler appeared in a note right below the one on Bill:

—The Swea City Herald notes the sudden death of James Kerwin of Winnebago in that place Tuesday night, Feb. 16th, of heart disease. His home was at Winnebago, where the wife and four children reside. His remains were shipped to Morris, this state, for interment.

—Ronald Weiler, who was so seriously injured a couple of weeks ago by coming in contact with a high voltage wire off a high line company near Decorah, had an arm amputated at the hospital at that place last week. The arm was taken off above the elbow. The loss of an eye from a like mishap last summer followed by this second accident will probably end his service with a high line repair crew. With other of his Blue Earth acquaintances, The Post regrets the young man's misfortune.

Somehow these two stories might have become intertwined in people's minds and the power-line accident used to explain my grandfather's early death. When I first was looking into Bill's death and finding no mention of an electric shock, I wondered if there couldn't possibly have been a cover-up by the power company, but after reading all these stories on the Weiler accident, it seemed unlikely. Bill Kirwin's obituary in the *Morris Sun* reported that my grandfather was "working with an electrical crew at the time of his death," which, if read incorrectly, could sound as if he was in the act of working when he died.

But this was all I could do with the mystery of my grandfather's death. After all, I have to wonder if he even died from heart failure. Wouldn't an autopsy have been indicated, even in 1926? Early deaths such as this were no longer common. Thinking about his death, I've concluded that possibly the family concocted the electric shock explanation in order to explain how he had come to die.

No one avoided the fact that he had died of a heart attack, but to protect themselves from this capricious death of the oldest son of eleven children and a father of four, they may have added the electric shock. After all, he did work on a power line. Something powerful must have happened to him, something extraordinary to bring him down like that. Surely not just a cold.

For me, this was the day that defined Mae Kirwin's life, that transformed her into the woman I came to know as my grandmother. Just as the weather could change dramatically in this middle-of-the-continent state, so could a life. A tight tunnel of a tornado whirled through her life and her husband was gone. Because of his death, she moved back to Chokio and got a full-time job. Mae never married again; she had no more children. She raised the five children she had with Bill Kirwin on her own.

I never heard my mother say anything about how their life might have been if her dad had lived. Although she hardly knew him, she still knew him better than any of the other children. If Bill had lived, there might well have been more children. Up to the time of his death, they were averaging a child a year. Bill came from a family of eleven children; Mae from a family of nine. Big families were still the norm in rural Minnesota.

But later, when speaking of our family, my mother would say that neither she nor my father knew what a father should do. Her father had died when she was almost five and my dad's father had been absent as well, drinking and traveling to other towns for work. Both my parents assumed that the women did it all—raised the children, ran the household, kept the family together. A woman managed on her own, as her mother had.

Mae called Bill's parents, Frank and Barbara Kirwin, and told them Bill had died. According to Grandma Carrie, they thought she was talking about the expected baby, who was to be called Bill if he was a boy, so they didn't respond as she thought they would. They assumed that the child would be buried in Winnebago and that there was nothing they could do. Finally they realized that it was Bill their son who had died. A family delegation—Bill's father, his sister, and her husband—went down to get Mae and the children and accompany the body back to Morris.

James William "Bill" Kirwin received a military funeral at Assumption Church in Morris, Minnesota, the Friday after he died. Then he was interred at Calvary Cemetery in Morris. The family put a thank-you note in the *Morris Sun* on Thursday, March 4. The note read:

Card of Thanks

We wish to express our most sincere thanks to all our friends and neighbors for every act of kindness and sympathy tendered us during our sad bereavement.

May God bless them all.
Mrs. Jas. W. Kirwin
Mr. and Mrs. F. J. Kirwin and Family
Mr. P. H. McNally

When I first read this note, for a moment I couldn't figure out who Mrs. Jas. W. Kirwin was. Then I realized it was Mae. This would be one of the last times she would be known by that name, for when a woman was widowed in those days in that part of the country, her name changed from "Mrs." Bill Kirwin, to "Mrs." Mae Kirwin. From this time on, Mae was referred to in the newspaper and other documents by her widowed name.

Mae stayed out at the Kirwin farm, a mile northwest of

Morris, until her baby was born. For the last month of her pregnancy, she was kept in bed because the Kirwin family feared that she might lose the baby. I was surprised that Mae wasn't in Chokio with her own family, but my aunt Pat explained that one of her husband's brothers, John Joseph Kirwin, was a gynecologist who would help deliver the baby. Mae's father Peter McNally went to move Mae's household effects from Winnebago to Chokio two weeks after her husband died.

On March 12, William Hugh Kirwin, named for his father and his mother's brother Hugh, came into the world. His birth at the Morris hospital was announced in the *Morris Tribune.* He, like his brother Jim, came to bear a striking resemblance to his father—dark, flashing eyes, short, stocky body, feisty but sunny personality. In all the pictures I have ever seen of him, he is smiling and staring openly at the camera.

This youngest of Mae's children had four older siblings—one brother and three sisters. My mother Ruthmary was the oldest. She turned five on the day of her father's funeral. It probably wasn't a very happy birthday for her. She was quite a small child, with big blue eyes, black straight hair, and fair skin—coloring she would always claim was the true Irish complexion.

James Peter turned four that May. As the older boy, he came to take on a lot of responsibility for the family. He was very active as a child and even though he wasn't any taller than five foot six, he loved all sports and played football in high school.

Patricia Marguerite Kirwin was only two when Bill was born. Her third birthday was that following June. She had curly, sandy blonde hair and dark brown eyes that snapped with life.

Helen Elaine Kirwin, the youngest girl, was known as Dutt all her life because she had dark brown hair that was

Kirwin family portrait, about 1939. Left to right: Helen "Dutt" Elaine, James Peter, Patricia Marguerite, Mae, William Hugh, Ruthmary.

cut in a little dutch boy cut. "Dutchy" became "Dutty" became "Dutt." She had turned one the October before Bill was born. Dutt had a split septum that was operated on several times later in her life. It caused her to have a rather squashed-looking nose and made her insecure about her looks.

⤛⤜

After Bill was born, Mae took her five children and moved back with her father Pete McNally in Chokio. Her only other sibling in Chokio at this time was Edna, who was married and had two children—one-year-old Robert and newborn Madonna. Shortly before Bill Kirwin's death, the value of his personal property was published with the tax roll in the *Winnebago City Press-News* on January 9, 1926: $483. So Mae had a little money, but it wouldn't have lasted her long with six mouths to feed. Times were tough on the prairie, and her father was sixty years old. He had retired from his position as postmaster in 1921. But he had a home and he shared it with his widowed daughter and her children.

The current postmaster, Fred A. Shipman, was up for reappointment. Mae had worked with her father in the post office for several years after she graduated from St. Mary's Academy. The McNally family were staunch Democrats and the position of postmaster was a political appointment. However, even though the Republicans were in power until 1931, a lawyer friend from Morris, Thomas Mangan, Jr., was able to pull some strings and get the appointment for Mae. Tom Mangan was also a state senator at this time. Later, he would handle Mae's sister Marguerite's divorce. As Donna Reichmuth explained to me, "Tom cashed in all his chits" to help Mae out.

Two years after her husband died, her youngest almost two years old, Mae Kirwin began work in February 1928 as the postmaster of Chokio, Minnesota. She held the position for nearly twenty years. In 1920, the federal census reported there were nearly 32,000 postmasters in the United States. About 21,000 were men and slightly over 11,000 were women. However, Mae Kirwin was and remains the only long-term woman postmaster of Chokio.

From 1926 to 1932, the position of postmaster of Chokio—a third-class post office—paid $1,700. To put this in perspective, in 1922 the average salary for a school teacher in Minnesota was $1,113. The annual salary was paid semimonthly and was based on the class of the post office. According to the pay scale for a postmaster in 1925, the Chokio post office must have been taking in between $2,700 and $3,000 a year. What could such a salary buy in 1927? A loaf of bread cost 10 cents, a pound of bacon was 47 cents, a quart of milk 14 cents, a pound of coffee 50 cents.

The McNally family had strong ties to the post office. In 1891 the second postmaster of the town had been Mae's

Mae Kirwin, postmaster of Chokio, 1938

uncle, James H. McNally. Then another uncle, the former newspaper owner Charles McAllen, was postmaster from 1914 to 1916. Mae's father Peter McNally ran it from 1916 to 1921. Mae was postmaster from 1928 until 1946. After her, a nephew, Jack Reichmuth, ran it for several years. Later, James F. McNally, another relative, would be postmaster for over twenty years. So for more than sixty years of the 105 years the position has existed, either Mae or someone related to her was in charge of the Chokio post office.

At this time the post office was open twelve hours a day—from six-thirty in the morning to six-thirty at night, six days a week. With such long hours, Mae relied on hired girls to tend the children. My aunt Pat has a vivid memory of their mother coming home from work: "We'd watch and watch for her. Our house was only two blocks from where she worked. In the winter time she wore an old fur coat of her mother's. It hung from the shoulders and it would billow out. She used to grab the front of it and wrap it around her. In the winter time when we'd go to meet her, we'd all get under this fur coat and just about trip her getting home."

With five small children and a full-time job, Mae needed help to run the household. By this time, Ruthmary and Jim attended school, but that still left the three youngest at home. One of the first girls she hired was a sixteen-year-old named Selma Larson.

While I was working on this book, Joanie McNally ran into Selma's sister at an auction near Chokio. They got talking in a friendly way and Joanie found out that Selma had worked for my grandmother and was still alive, residing in Michigan. Joanie gave me her address and I quickly wrote her, then waited for a reply. I had no idea what shape Selma was in, if she would in fact be able to answer any of my questions, but I hoped. I so wanted a sense of my grandmother at this point in her life.

Three weeks after I wrote to her, I received a reply from Mrs. Selma Gillies. She was now about eighty-one years old. She praised my grandmother and reported that she was very easy to work for and also very caring. "Now that I look back, Mae was way ahead of her time. She wasn't the cookie-making kind of mother but she was caring. And she was very good to the girls that worked for her. . . . I believe a book on Mae could be very interesting."

Selma had gone to work because her father died and she had been forced to leave school. She described the Depression as "hard times but to me they were also my happy years." She gave me short but accurate statements about the Kirwin children from the time she knew them:

Ruth very stubborn
Jim easy going
Toddy [she means Dutty]—my love

Pat never knew what she would get into
Billy a doll

Later, I called my aunt Pat and read her Selma's short profiles. She laughed and said she thought that Selma just about got it right. Pat went on to say that Ruthmary was spunky, Jim a tease, she herself was sassy, Dutty was always very quiet, and all that she could remember about Bill was that Momma babied him.

When she was first postmaster, Mae had to meet the early Morris-to-Browns-Valley bus to pick up the mail. In the 1930s, the train, nicknamed the "Toonerville Trolley" after a popular newspaper cartoon, started carrying the mail.

In Chokio in the 1930s and 1940s, the post office was the communication center. There was no UPS. All packages came through the mail. Long-distance phone service was expensive and complicated to use. People corresponded through letters and picked up their mail in person unless they were on a rural route. This made the post office a general gathering spot. People not only learned news from afar at the post office, but local gossip circulated there also.

One of the busiest times for the Chokio post office was when the Sears Roebuck and Montgomery Ward catalogs arrived. Mae's children went down to help her sort them. The catalogs filled numerous mail sacks. Because of their weight and size, only a certain number could be filed in the boxes at a time or they would pull the mail racks down. So the children would line most of them up on the desk and write the recipients' names on the spine of the catalogs and put a card in their box. Sometimes it took up to a week to get all the catalogs unsacked, addressed, filed, and distributed to the people.

I visited the post office in Chokio, but all the records of Mae's years there had been destroyed. However, I found a description of the job of a postal clerk, Marlys Alm, from

Donnelly, a town close to Chokio, in *An Honest Day's Work,*
published by the Stevens County Historical Society:

> There were no trucks either bringing in or picking up the
> mail when day was done, so each morning you picked the
> mail bags up from the depot, put them on a cart, and
> pushed, pulled or however, across the railroad track through
> snow, mud, and water puddles to the post office. This was
> an early morning duty—then the mail was sorted and
> placed in the patron's boxes. Not everyone rented a box so
> the rest was handed out as General Delivery. We had many
> early customers, especially to get their newspapers. We had
> a few Wall Street Journal subscribers anxious to check on
> the market. . . .
>
> At the end of the day the mail was bagged, and second
> class and parcels taken to the depot to be picked up during
> the night by the local train. The first class mail was bagged
> and locked to be taken to a pole by the track where you
> climbed up and hung this bag on a hook—a rather hairy job
> when it was 30–40 below or hot, hot in summer and slip-
> pery when wet. You stood on one leg and stretched a mile.
> The fast mail train came along and grabbed this bag with
> a hook. When they missed you had to climb up again and
> take the bag down and put it in the depot. Only once when
> I worked was it broken open so the mail was scattered at
> least a half mile down the right of way.

While I was writing this section on the post office, I suddenly remembered a piece my mother had written looking
back on Chokio and the post office where she had worked
with her mother. She sent it to me and I, unlike the rest of
my extended family, had saved that letter.

> In cities there are certain "types" of people, but in the small
> town they are "characters." One such was Uncle Jim, he
> hadn't worked much since he was forty (but his wife and
> kids were all good hard workers). Now in his sixties, he liked

to go hunting with his 'dags' or sit in front of the Post Office with his hearing aid turned off and his false teeth in his pocket and watch the world go by.

This bench in front of the post-office is a favorite sitting spot for some of the old codgers around town, since every one stops in there at least once a day to pick up the mail. There is no home delivery in the whole town. The village constable can be found there pretty often. He turns the town water pump on at certain intervals so the villagers will have water. Another of his duties is to turn on the fire siren at noon so the citizenry will know it's time to eat dinner (they have supper in the evening) and again at nine o'clock in the evening to get the kids off the streets. These are known as the noon whistle and curfew. His peacekeeping duties are practically non-existent, but one Saturday night he put a couple of the town rowdies in the local jail until they sobered up, but most of the time he just walks around and touches his hat to those he meets or sits in front of the post-office.

Then there is Indian Joe. No one seems to know why he is so called, since he isn't an Indian—maybe he lived on the Indian reservation at one time, who knows. He came to Chokio some years ago from over near there, and he settled down to live out his life in sem-enebriation. He is never really drunk, but he's not completely sober either.

Most mornings between nine and ten o'clock these three worthies will be found on their favorite bench, watching their neighbors stop by to pick the mail.

Sometimes their vigil is rewarded. Something important happens. Like the time Mike Mahoney was a little late picking up his mail and Mr. T. Eugene Howe was a little early. These arch enemies met right in front of the watchers. Mr. Howe (always the formal gentleman) tipped his hat and said, "Good morning, Mr. Mahoney." and Mike (a cantankerous old Irishman) said, "Good morning, Mr. Howe." but, as he turned to go in the door, he turned back and said, "Say, I'd like it if you wouldn't say 'good Morning' to me nor wish me the time o' day. It wouldn't hurt you none, and it would help me like hell." and he stalked away.

The watchers looked knowingly at one another and each made some excuse for having to get home. By shopping time that afternoon everyone in town knew that Mike and Old Howe had finally revealed their animosity. The weekly newspaper is for births and deaths, but the real living news of the village comes on the buzz-line.

〜※〜

In 1929, Mae moved out of her father's home and bought her own house two blocks away. The one-story house with no basement had been previously owned by a Mr. and Mrs. Moffatt. There were three bedrooms, a kitchen, a living room, a dining room, and a screened-in front porch. Pat remembers workmen jacking up the house around 1930 with a team of horses and then putting a basement under it. Mae lived in this small clapboard house the rest of her life.

A few years after I bought a small white farmhouse down on Lake Pepin and planted hollyhocks all along the south side of the house, I found an old picture of my grandmother's house. It shocked me how closely I had replicated it: with their white clapboard and hollyhocks, the two houses were almost identical on their south sides, except that my house was two storeys.

〜※〜

I've always thought of the Depression as starting in 1929—the horrible "Black Thursday" stock market crash of October 24. But for the farmers in western Minnesota and North and South Dakota, there hadn't been much of a roaring twenties. Grain prices had dropped off in the early 1920s when Europe no longer needed to buy food from America. In July 1920, wheat sold at Minneapolis for $2.96 a bushel. By 1922, it had fallen to 92 cents. By 1930, it had tumbled to 36 cents.

Mae was appointed postmaster at a time when any job looked good to a hungry family. She certainly never would have been given that job over a man if she hadn't been supporting her own family of five children. Stevens County was one of the hardest hit counties in Minnesota, according to historian D. Jerome Tweton. "Counties in west-central Minnesota to the south of Wilkin were not spared the drought and grasshoppers which also ravaged the Dakotas. These wheat counties . . . fell victim to the 'Dakota drought,' which wiped out hundreds of farmers in Big Stone, Stevens, Pope and Swift counties."

At this time, one-third of the population of Minnesota lived either on farms or in villages like Chokio that were dependent on the farm dollar. Mae was lucky—she was not paid by the village. She was a federal employee and as such was able to keep her children in clothes.

The Depression started early in Chokio and lasted throughout most of the 1930s. This era formed my mother and her siblings. Even after my father was making a good salary at 3M in St. Paul, my mother sewed her own clothes and always liked to get a bargain. She told me stories about what it was like growing up during this time. Through her off-hand comments, I saw the paucity of their material life. One day she told me that she didn't have bubble gum as a child; instead, she would chew on the tar that was used to hold the shingles on the roof.

My mother told me how the dust of the 1930s, stirred up by the high winds, sifted down on everything. Her mother made all the children line up wet washrags on the window ledges to keep the dust from easing through the sills, but it would get in anyway. As Lois Phillips Hudson wrote in *Reapers of the Dust:* "Dust storms are like that: no matter how many times you clean or how much you scrub and repaint and dig into crevices, you are always finding another niche the dust has found. And in the dust is the smell of mortality, of fertility swept away and spring vanished." This dust was the fertile topsoil blown off the farmland all around them.

My aunt Pat remembers those summers of the 1930s when the wind blew and there was no rain for months: "I recall mother would let us wear our underpanties around home on weekends when she was there. We'd strip down to our underpanties and she'd bring a small fan, which nobody had in those days, home from the post office on Saturday nights and we would get to lay on the floor in front of the fan on Sunday afternoons."

When I drove out to Chokio with my mother in later years, she pointed out the lines of trees marching down the land near farmhouses. "Windbreaks," she said fiercely. "You need trees as windbreaks out here." Farmers fought a war with the land, and those seemingly ornamental trees were evidence of their battles.

But the story from my mother's childhood during the Depression that made the most lasting impression on me was about reading books. She told me that when she was a child, Chokio had no library. Every family had a few books, but they were very valuable and not to be lent out. So in order to read a book, my mother had to go over to a neighbor's house and sit on their front porch to read it. Her mother gave her firm instructions not to stay till suppertime, because, as she explained, "They might think they have to invite you to stay for supper, and they don't have enough food to feed you."

❧

Chokio during the late 1920s and 1930s offered few cultural and social activities. Mae didn't own a car, so she could travel only if she rode along with someone else or took the train. The children must have kept her at home when she wasn't working. But people visited: whole families would walk over to a neighbor's house and sit and visit. My mother visited all her life.

Visiting consisted simply of going to someone's house for coffee during the day or maybe a beer at night (during the years of Prohibition, 1920 to 1933, a homebrew). Usually a fair number of cigarettes were smoked. An elbow leaned on a counter. Gossip and the condition of the world were discussed. Mae was a good visitor when she had a chance. According to many of her friends, she especially excelled in this activity once she had retired from the post office. But I don't doubt that she squeezed in a little visiting on most weekends during her working years.

People also entertained themselves at home. The Kirwin family was very musical; Mae played the piano and everyone sang. In later years, my mother worked as a singing waitress to put herself through college. Mae liked her children to bring their friends over. They would have a taffy pull. They would make popcorn. Mae played the piano. They would push back the table in the dining room and all dance. Mae taught her children to dance and this, too, stood my mother in good stead, for she later taught dancing at Arthur Murray and showed my whole Girl Scout troop how to waltz and foxtrot.

Christmas was the big midwinter celebration, and the Mae Kirwin family always spent it at home. Mae worked all day long on Christmas Eve, making sure the townspeople received their packages before the holiday. Then she would make her way home so the hired girl could leave for her own family celebration.

Aunt Pat described what went on when Mae arrived home: "We kids always had a program for mom. We'd worked on it many days while she was at work. We sang and recited poems. Then at the end Mother would play piano and we'd all sing Christmas carols. When we were small, we'd have

Christmas on Christmas morning. Mother would go to midnight Mass and then come home and we'd all get up in the morning. One year she went to midnight Mass and when she came home Santa had already been there and all the presents were open. So from then on we had Christmas on Christmas Eve and then we all went to midnight Mass."

One Christmas Mae bought the whole family a radio. A man came out on Christmas Eve afternoon and hooked the aerial up. That year they listened to Christmas Eve programs on the radio. Aunt Pat recalled that the hired girls enjoyed the radio too. When Mae went to play bridge, the hired girls sat and smooched in front of the radio with their boyfriends while the Kirwin children peeked at them.

<hr>

This family had an odd consciousness about having only one parent. If anything happened to Mae, how would they manage? Aunt Pat described how they all felt: "Mom was the center of our home and our lives, and everything that went on in our family. We didn't have two parents to turn to, we only had one. And I'm sure each and every one of us kids did our own little worrying that something would happen to Mom before we were grown up."

Once Ruthmary reached high school, the family no longer needed a hired girl. When the school day was over, Mae's children stopped by the post office to see what they should make for dinner. Then they would go home, clean up the lunch dishes, and get dinner.

The usual childhood calamities befell them. Pat broke her leg when a motorcycle fell over on her and Jim broke a leg playing football in high school. They all got the mumps. But as they grew up, they were better able to help their mother around the house and in the post office.

Ruthmary started working in the post office with Mae

when she was around fourteen years old. In seventh grade, Pat worked at the grocery store owned by her father's brother, blind uncle George, and her aunt Jean. Uncle George and Aunt Jean lived above their Red Owl store. One morning the store caught on fire and the volunteer fire department was called out. It took them all day to put out the fire, cutting holes in the roof and pouring in water. At about four o'clock, Uncle George stood in the middle of the mess, said, "to heck with everything," and, reported my aunt Pat, "got all snockered up."

Jim worked part-time at the hardware store through most of high school. After he graduated, he worked there full time. The owner of the store even sent him on to plumbing school.

My aunt Pat told me two good stories about my mother from these times. One summer Ruthmary and Pat went to Grandma Kirwin's in Morris for a few weeks. Uncle Ed let them ride into the field on the manure spreader and watch him fertilize, and then they got to ride in the back end with the barley, right up to the barn. That same day Grandma gave them some dried beans in a sack to put in their suitcase to take home with them. Ruthmary kept singing, "Beans in the suitcases and barley in the pants."

Then, one day when all the kids were playing next door at the Ravers' house, Mae hollered out, "Ruthie!" Nothing happened. Then she called, "Ruth-mary," but still nothing. Mrs. Raver said to Ruth, "Ruthmary, your mother is calling you." Just then Mae called out, "Ruthmary Kirwin." "Oh," Ruthmary said as she heard her mother enunciate her full name. "Now it's time to go."

The family had a Scottish terrier called Scotty during these years. I've often wondered if Mae had one because FDR had one. Scotty was really Mae's dog. He went to work with Mae, lay under her desk, went home at noon, went back to work at one o'clock, and then came home in the evening. On

Sundays he even went to church with Mae and waited outside until she came out. One workday in winter, there was a bad snowstorm, and Mae came home without Scotty. She told the kids that he just couldn't make it through the snow. His little short legs couldn't handle the snowbanks. The snow was too soft and he was mired under. So Jim had to bundle up and go down to the post office and carry him home that day.

Through this middle part of her life, Mae Kirwin continued to follow the traditions of the Irish—she remained steadfast to the Catholic church and she was a fierce Democrat. She was also active, during the 1930s, in the postmasters' organizations, both at the state and national level. Outside of her children, her work, her religion, and her political party formed her social activities.

Mae Kirwin went to church at St. Mary's, also known as Our Lady of Perpetual Help. The first church in Chokio, it was built in 1897 with the help of Mae's two aunts—Mrs. Jim and Mrs. Mike McNally. According to the *Chokio Community History*, "Mrs. Jim, who was pregnant, and Mrs. Mike taking along her three month old baby, canvassed the whole rural community, with horses and buggy and organized a big picnic dinner, for the 4th of July 1895 at the grain elevator." This "kick-off" event was the first of many fund-raising activities. A fair in October netted $600. The Joseph Shannon Company of Graceville built the church and parish house.

Parish priests came and stayed in Chokio. From 1907 to 1924, the Reverend John Hengarten served at St. Mary's. He was the priest who married Mae and Bill. The Reverend Felix Reimers was priest there from 1926 to 1933. He might have baptized young Bill, and he certainly gave First Communion to most of Mae's children. Then from 1933 to 1944,

Reverend Henry Leuthner was in residence. I heard from several people that this priest had a wonderful relationship with Mae's scottie dog, feeding him scraps on the side.

These parish priests had immense power in Chokio. When my mother talked of her wedding, she always mentioned how the priest had threatened to excommunicate my grandmother if she went to my mother's wedding in a Lutheran church. My parents almost didn't marry because of their different religions. My cousin claims that his mother, my mother's sister, was excommunicated. To me as a child, this sounded like a fearful thing. But then being raised Lutheran by my father, I found much that the Catholics did sounded awful.

As Andrew Greeley explained in his book on the Irish in America, "Unquestionably, the parish priest is a man of great, but limited, power. . . . The loyalty to the priest and the parish, whether in Ireland or America, is a symbol of the fact that one is Irish and Catholic." I heard this loyalty whenever any of my Catholic relatives talked about their church; it made me feel as if my family was outsiders.

My grandmother took me to her church, but I understood I wasn't to let my parents know. No one ever came right out and told me this, but I knew my parents wouldn't approve of my going to a Catholic church, especially my father. When I went to stay with Grandma, my mother didn't send a hat along with me, and in 1959 no woman could enter a Catholic church with her head uncovered. Mae scurried around to the neighbors' to find me a hat. I don't know what my parents thought she was going to do with me while she was at church. I don't remember the church well; at that time the service must have been in Latin, which I don't recall, but I do remember the search for the hat. Wearing a borrowed hat, like a disguise, made churchgoing illicit and exciting.

When I began looking into my grandmother's life, I found several mysteries that I wanted to try to solve. I use the word *try* here with much thought. In digging into the past, one has to rely heavily on chance—will the right person remember the right thing, will the document that contains the desired information come to light? But in researching I have found that perseverance and a certain deviousness of mind aided me more than I would have imagined.

One of the mysteries of my grandmother's life was that she had a boyfriend. When I was in my thirties and driving my mother to Chokio for her fiftieth high-school reunion, my mother told me something about my grandmother that I would never have guessed. By then, my mother had suffered a stroke and had lost much of her ability to tell stories, but occasionally tales did bubble up. I must have asked her something about Mae, and she answered that Grandma had had a boyfriend. Mom remembered one Christmas when this boyfriend had sent a huge box with presents to all the Kirwin children. My mom was in her early teens then. She said that he had asked Mae to marry him, but she turned him down because he wasn't Catholic. I believed my mother and asked no more about him, which I have since regretted. I think of the empty miles we drove in western Minnesota that could have been filled with more information about this mystery man.

But I've been determined to find him, this man who courted my grandmother. In some ways I found the idea of him more interesting than that of my own grandfather, possibly because here was the hint of romance in a life that I thought had contained little. Also, my grandmother had met him when she was in her early forties, which is the age I am now, and I wondered if I, too, would have found him attractive.

The first clue about this man's identity came in a packet of photocopies sent to me by my cousin Don. It was a photocopy of a card with my grandmother's picture on it and someone else's name written underneath. The year was 1934; Mae would have been forty years old. The card was a Short Term Press Pass for the Century of Progress International Exposition, a big world fair held in Chicago. In the photograph, my grandmother was smiling, a fur collar draped around her neck and a hat tilted sideways. She was a large, healthy woman who looked as if she was having a lot of fun. But on the pass her name was given as Mrs. Roy Swanson and the "account" was listed as Budget–Bronson, Minn. Mae signed the card as Mrs. Ray R. Swanson. Above the photocopy, my cousin Don had written that Mae was "using name of boyfriend to get pass."

Easy enough: her boyfriend was Ray or Roy Swanson from Bronson, Minnesota. I decided his name was Ray because I didn't think Mae would make a mistake. But the current map of Minnesota showed no Bronson, Minnesota. Later, at the Minnesota History Center, I looked at *Minnesota Geographic Names* and found that there had been a Bronson, Minnesota, in 1934. The name of the town was later changed to Lake Bronson when a river was dammed to form the lake.

When I found out where Bronson was, I faced yet another mystery. Bronson is up in the northwest corner of Minnesota in Kittson County, some twenty miles from the Canadian border but about 220 miles from Chokio. As far as I knew, Mae had no connection with that part of the state. I had never heard my mother mention any trips there. So how had she met Mr. Swanson?

And how was I to find Mr. Swanson? The census for Bronson was only available up to 1920, and when I checked it, I didn't find a Ray Swanson. I also tried to find out what "Budget" was. I assumed it was some sort of business, but I was overlooking an important clue. Finally, I decided to try the newspaper. Most small towns—and Bronson at 240 was small—had newspapers. I was elated to find that the newspaper was called the *Bronson Budget* and that Mr. Ray R. Swanson was one of its publishers.

I still didn't understand how he and Mae had come to know each other, but that soon was made clear when I read that he was also the postmaster of Bronson. On October 10, 1934, Mr. Ray Swanson, the state secretary-treasurer for the District Postmasters of Minnesota, left for the national convention held that year in Columbus, Ohio. A small piece in the *Bronson Budget* said that this was the third convention Swanson had gone to and that he drove from St. Paul in the company of "other Minnesota postmasters."

I read through several months of *Bronson Budget*s before I finally found the article that clinched it, explaining in great detail how Ray and Mae had met. The January 3, 1935, headline read: "Bronson Postmaster Writes Account of Trip to National Convention." After all, Swanson was also one of the newspaper's publishers. He could write about whatever he wanted to:

> Having written an account of two previous trips to national conventions of postmasters, and at the request of a large number of postmasters and local friends although somewhat belated, I shall here in my humble way endeavor to give an account of the trip made this fall to the National Convention of the League of District Postmasters of the United States held at Columbus, Ohio on October 16-17-18-19.

Swanson gave a blow-by-blow account of this trip. He left Bronson on October 10 with his mother and sister, both of whom he was taking to St. Paul. He described the day: "It was a typical, clear, sunny Minnesota fall day with the azure blue sky in all its glory. Enroute to the cities we noticed potato digging, plowing and shocking corn as the general order of farming." In his inflated style, he wrote of a visit to the new St. Paul post office:

Postmaster Van Dyke assigned Mr. Preston to escort Mr. Omholt, Mr. Hanson and the writer through the beautiful $2,450,000 structure. In fact the building is so highly admired that while we were in Dr. Van Dyke's office word came that a Chicago architectural firm had a photographer on the street taking a $350 photo of the building for a magazine, it having been selected as one of the outstanding in the nation.

At the bottom of the story's first column, on the front page of the *Bronson Budget,* my grandmother entered the picture:

On Friday morning at 8:20 we set out on our journey to Chicago, with one addition to the above named in the person of Postmaster Mrs. Mae Kirwin of Chokio, who was going as a delegate to the Columbus Convention and then continue on to Baltimore, Maryland, for a visit with her sister.

The sister was twenty-nine-year-old Marguerite, who was married to John Mordica by this time.

The convention-goers made it to Chicago the first night and Swanson told of the sights: "Arriving in Chicago late at night we could not help but notice the contrast between the contented farming region we had passed through as compared to gayly flickering lights of the night clubs and taverns of Cicero and other suberbs, where we often hear someone has been shot for less than a nickel."

The next day they all went to the Century of Progress exposition (we know how Mae gets into it), and Swanson raved ecstatically about it:

This great exposition commemorating the one-hundredth anniversary of the rise of Chicago from a small settlement to the fourth largest in the world was indeed interesting. It would require columns to describe even a small portion of the Fair. The exhitibition features the service of science to humanity, progress made in the arts and sciences and every phase of human existence as developed in the last one hundred years. The architectural designs, lighting effects and other startling innovations were indeed beautiful. Every moment there was something to see and admire. After wearing out a generous amount of shoe leather hoofing from one end of the grounds to the other we rolled in for the night.

In Plymouth, Indiana, the next day, the travelers "encountered our first and only flat tire." This flat tire was of special interest to me because my grandmother also possessed pictures of this trip that were passed on to my aunt Pat. One picture showed Mae in front of the Plymouth post office. On the back of the picture Mae wrote, "The only Picture of its kind in existance." What she was referring to was the sight of Republican Ray R. Swanson standing to the right of her in front of the Democratic headquarters.

Mae also had a picture of what she called the "bunch" from "Minnesota National Convention at Columbus, Ohio, 1934." In this picture, she and three men were standing in front of what must have been Swanson's automobile, a Ford. Again, Ray Swanson was the man to her right, the tallest of the three gentlemen. They were all dressed in suits and two of them had on vests. All of them were wearing hats. Mae had on a jaunty-looking hat and a midcalf coat. She was wearing tie shoes with a slight heel. In one hand she carried a clutch bag and a pair of gloves. Fairly fashionable, but quite businesslike.

These two pictures of Swanson surprised me. He looked quite a bit younger than Mae. In reading his account of his trip to the convention, I didn't much like his tone of voice. I didn't completely approve of him as Mae's suitor. Then, on top of that, he was Republican and Lutheran—certainly not a perfect fit.

The party drove into Columbus, which had a population at the time of 340,400 people; Mr. Ray Swanson did like his figures. He went on to say that 94.7 percent of the people

*An unidentified man,
Mae Kirwin, and Ray
Swanson, Plymouth,
Indiana, 1934*

were reported to be American-born and that there were 533 manufacturing plants in the city.

Finally, the convention. Postmaster Swanson was concise about the event:

> The twenty-ninth annual convention of the National League of District Postmasters opened at the Deshler-Wallick Hotel Tuesday morning and continued through to Friday. Delegates were present from practically every state in the union, representing some 43,000 third and fourth class postmasters. Minnesota was represented by the following postmasters: A. C. Omholt, Sacred Heart; Norman Hanson, Renville; Mae Kirwin, Chokio; Ralph C. Peterson, Dilworth; Freda M. Levin, Zim; Svend Peterson, Askov and Ray R. Swanson. The writer had the honor and pleasure of giving the response to the adresses of welcome at the opening ses-

sion, attempting to properly convey the sentiments of the many delegates who had assembled from all parts of the United States.

The governor of Ohio and the mayor of Columbus were among the many speakers at the four-day conference. Swanson reported that "The ladies in attendance enjoyed a reception and tea at the Governor's Mansion, with Miss White as hostess." After the conference was over, the Minnesota delegation made a tour of the city, then left the next day to travel back to Minnesota, while Mae instead traveled on to visit Marguerite in Maryland.

The Minnesotans stopped at the Indiana birthplace of poet James Whitcomb Riley, and Swanson was moved enough to write a tribute: "We took a picture in front of Riley's home and I was inspired to write the following if you would call it a poem." In this piece, Swanson explained why he so admired Riley: "We have always admired Mr. Riley / As a poet grand / One who wrote verse / that was easy to understand."

The next time I know for sure that Mae and Ray were together was on June 20–21, 1935, at a postmasters' convention in Bemidji. Of course, the *Bronson Budget* featured a big article on it with quite a nice photo of Postmaster Ray R. Swanson, hair parted right down the middle and slicked back tight.

According to Swanson's report, the convention was held at the Bemidji armory with badges furnished through the courtesy of Montgomery Ward & Co. The meeting was called to order at 10 A.M. by the state president, followed by the advance of colors, pledge to the flag, and singing of "The Star Spangled Banner." A few more songs and a couple more welcomes and the next two speakers were "Response—Ray R. Swanson, P.M. Bronson. Report of the 29th National Convention, Colombus, Ohio—Mae A Kirkwin, Postmaster, Chokio."

I couldn't believe that Swanson did not spell Mae's name correctly in his own paper. But I'm glad of the evidence that they were once again together. And each night of the convention there was a dance; Thursday it was the Postmasters Grand Annual Ball in the ballroom, featuring "Birchmont Hotel Music by Joe Plummers Orchestra. Modern and Old Time Music" with "Special Entertainment Features." The next night was simply the "Postmasters' Dance" at the Shorecrest Pavilion.

An announcement in Swanson's paper not even a month later, on July 11, 1935, shocked me. Then I thought I understood. The headline read: "Local Postmaster Married July 4th." The article continued:

> A marriage of interest to Kittson County folks occured on American's greatest of holidays, July 4th, when Ray R. Swanson, local postmaster, left the ranks of the bachelors and took a bride. . . .
>
> Helen Harriet [Anderson] is a product of Kittson County and is one of the popular young ladies of Hallock where she has continually made her home.
>
> The groom needs no introduction to the readers of the Budget as he is one of the co-publishers of this paper, together with serving as postmaster of Bronson a number of years. He has always been one of our most active and influential businessmen and the holder of many honorary positions.
>
> The newlyweds are now nicely located in their cozy bungalow on Main street where they will continue to enjoy the warm friendship of the people of this village.
>
> The people of this county join with fellow workers and a host of friends in extending sincere best wishes for a most happy and prosperous wedded life.

I could swear that Mr. Swanson wrote this article himself. It certainly bore his florid style. Then I began to fill in the gaps. I figured that Swanson had been pressing Mae to marry him and, when she turned him down, he rebounded to the next available woman and ran off with her. As I read on a bit further in the *Bronson Budget,* I noted that the October 10 issue mentioned that the Swansons went to the postmasters' national convention in Atlanta, Georgia, and that Ray had promised to write another account of the trip for the *Budget.* At least now I would be spared reading that.

Feeling quite proud of myself, I called my aunt Pat and told her that I had found Mae's boyfriend.

"Oh, really," she said.

"Yes: Ray Swanson from Bronson."

There was silence, and then she said, "That doesn't sound right. I thought he was from Mankato. He owned the paper."

"Ray Swanson owned the paper."

"No, his name was Fritz or Fitz. Mike Fritz."

"Oh," I said.

"Yes," she said. "I clearly remember the Christmas he sent us kids all brand-new snowsuits, Hudson Bay snowsuits. Those were expensive. I'll never forget that."

"How did they meet?"

"I think it was the Democratic convention."

"OK, thanks." I got off the phone and decided I might have found the wrong boyfriend. So I geared myself up for another search.

⟡

Mankato is a midsize river town in southern Minnesota. Located seventy-five miles south and slightly west of Minneapolis, it was founded where the Minnesota River takes a sharp turn north and heads up to the Twin Cities to join the Mississippi. If my grandmother had driven a little over twenty miles south of her house in Chokio and then boated down the Minnesota River about 120 miles, she would have arrived in Mankato. But I don't think she ever did that.

Once again, I had to find a man and then figure out how my grandmother might have met him.

Michael D. Fritz wasn't too hard to find. In 1937, the *Mankato Free Press* was fifty years old and published a big anniversary jubilee edition with a large article about its vice president. At this time, Fritz was not a young man. Born in 1868, he was sixty-nine in 1937; Mae was forty-three. I thought he was a bit old for her, but as I read about him, I warmed to him.

> From Ohio to South Dakota Mr. Fritz followed the printing trade in an early day. Born at Sandusky, O., the fifth of a family of seven children, he crossed the ocean to Germany with his mother when he was a lad six years old and was left an orphan in an Ohio town a few years later.
>
> At Elyria, O., a short distance from Cleveland, Fritz

Mae, about 1940

started his apprenticeship in the printing trade, working for $1 a week, limiting his one real meal of the week to Sunday. From Elyria he went to Fremont and from there to Estellin, S.D., where he worked on the Bell, a weekly which was sold by Fred Carruth, later a humorist on the New York Tribune staff, to Frank Parsons, father of Mrs. Harry Kelly of Mankato.

Starting a paper at Castlewood with equipment purchased in deferred payments on which the interest was 36 per cent a year, Mr. Fritz married a girl at Elyria in 1890. Mrs. Fritz died in March, 1919.

I was relieved to know that Mrs. Fritz had died long before Mae and Fritz had met. The article went on to list many of the organizations Mr. Fritz had been a member of: Minneopa Park board, city council, and Elks Club, to name a few.

But as I gathered more information about Mr. Fritz, I again became concerned about how he and Mae had met. The *Mankato Free Press* in the 1930s was very Republican, as was Mr. Fritz. According to his biography in *History of Blue Earth County,* "Mr. Fritz has always voted the Republican ticket straight. While in South Dakota he was secretary of the Republican County Committee." I also learned that the Fritzes had one daughter, Mildred, who was a year younger than Mae.

How then had Michael D. Fritz come to be at a Democratic convention? Possibly covering it for the paper, but I didn't think he wrote for the paper—he managed it. But I was sure he was the man. The more I learned about him, the more he fit the memories. My aunt Pat remembered him sending Mae the most enormous boxes of gladioli, which he had grown in his garden, and in his obituary in the *Mankato Free Press,* his garden was mentioned: "His extensive gladioli garden in Tincomville was among his chief interests in recent years. During the season when the flowers were in bloom he supplied generous bouquets for civic events and to business firms and his friends." And to my grandmother.

The *Mankato Free Press* published a small tribute to him after his death in 1941 that I found very touching, especially a paragraph describing his gardening ability:

There was the mark of the creative artist in Mike Fritz—if he had been a painter he would have gone in for great murals. He never did things by halves. A few years back he built two homes out in Oak Knoll. The houses were more or less incidental to him—the beautification of the grounds was a creative joy. Back of the house was a steep hillside, wooded and rough. . . . "I'm going to have a stairway running up here, landings along the way, a rustic gate at the top—and on the hillside, tulips, thousands of them." He saw the picture—none of the rest of us did until the next spring. The stairway in white, the rustic gate above, and 10,000 blooming tulips transformed that barren hillside into a wonderland as though Aladdin had rubbed his magic lamp. . . . Mike wasn't surprised. He knew it would look that way. While others came to gaze and wonder he labored, cutting the tulips and carrying them away to hospitals, pubic lobbies, friends and acquaintances who knew his unlimited generosity with flowers. All of his gardening and landscaping, and he did much of it, was on that same grand, sweeping scale.

I liked him—he sounded like a wonderful man. I could see why Mae had liked him, too, but how had they met? I had dinner with Mae's niece Donna Reichmuth and asked her about Mike Fritz. She vaguely remembered the name and then when I said he was from Mankato and that I was puzzled about how they had met, she said, "They met at the Democratic convention."

"That's what Aunt Pat says too. But he was Republican."

"Yes, but the convention was in Mankato."

That did it. Now all I had to do was track down the convention. I went back to the Minnesota History Center determined to find out when this convention had taken place. I expected my task would be easy: I would simply ask for the list of Democratic conventions, which take place every two years, and find out the year one was held in Mankato during the 1930s. What I discovered was that there was no written history of the Minnesota Democratic party before the 1940s.

The Democratic party came to Minnesota in 1849, six years before the Republicans, but the Republicans held power in Minnesota until near the turn of the century, when John Lind was elected governor. Then, in 1918, the first Farmer-Labor candidate ran for office. In 1944, after splitting many tickets, the Farmer-Labor party joined forces with the Democrats. A wonderful history of this party, *Worthy to Be Remembered,* tracks the party from 1944 to 1984. But it contains no list of party conventions.

So I went back to the newspapers. I searched through 1932, 1934, and 1936. I didn't think Mae and Fritz would have met much later than that because Aunt Pat thought she had been twelve years old when Fritz sent the children the snowsuits. After much digging, I found that the 1932 Democratic convention was held in St. Paul, no convention was held in 1934, and in 1936, to my great disappointment, the convention had been held in St. Cloud. And I had been so sure that it was in 1936 they had met!

But as I kept reading the *Mankato Free Press,* I came across a reference to the *other* Democratic state convention that had been held on February 1, 1936, in Mankato. I quickly pulled the February first issue of the paper and the headline across the top of the front page reads: "State Demos Instruct for Roosevelt." Subheads continue: "26 Delegates are First Instructed to Back President—Ryan Named Chairman of Meeting; Likely to Succeed Wolf—Over 2,000 Crowd Sessions at Armory—Endorsing Convention Likely in April to Pick State Ticket."

Minnesota became the first state in the union to instruct its delegates to endorse President Franklin D. Roosevelt. John E. Regan addressed the delegates and spoke strongly in support of the president:

> In the White House in Washington there sits a man, who in the last three years, has been called upon to meet problems, the like of which have never been presented to any president. He, too, is waiting to hear the result of this convention. He has waged a great battle for the common man. He might have sat among "the gods of wealth" and listened to their acclaim as did his predecessor, and those who would condemn him now. True to his promise, he listened to, and heard the cry of the oppressed, and he went out upon the highways; he gave rest to the weary; he fed the hungry, and clothed the naked.
>
> He came out into this great northwest and for the first time in the history of the nation, he gave relief to that class who toiled from sun up to sun down. He restored farms and homes to the destitute. Yes, my friends, . . . he is waiting for our message today.

But how could I find out if Mae Kirwin had actually been at the convention? It made sense to me that Fritz would attend this convention held in his town, if only out of curiosity. Because the Chokio newspapers for this time have been lost, I had to go back to the Morris papers, assuming they would tell me who went to the convention.

As I read through the January 3, 1936, issue of the *Morris Sun,* Mary Logue popped up again. She was forty years older than the first time I had read about her, and her name still startled me. The news item read: "Former Resident Hurt in Montana Accident. Mrs. George Stinson, formerly Mary Logue of this city, was critically injured in an automobile accident near Billings, Mont., on December 24th." She had managed to thread her way back into my story. Was I being poked again, reminded that this search for Mae somehow ended up being about me in the end? The jolt was there.

On Saturday, January 25, 1936, the Stevens County Democratic committee met in a courtroom in Morris. I scanned the article in the January 31 issue of the *Morris Sun* to find out who was chosen as a delegate to the state convention and was sorely disappointed when my grandmother's name was not among the delegates. But on a quick second read, I spied a name that gave me hope: Albert Reichmuth of Chokio was a delegate, and he was Mae's brother-in-law, Edna's husband. I thought there was a good chance that Mae was at the meeting. The committee adopted these resolutions:

> We the Democrats of Stevens county, in convention assembled, do hereby endorse the New Deal which includes the AAA and we instruct our delegates to the state convention a[t] Mankato to work and vote for the election of delegates to the national convention who will in turn vote for the nomination of Franklin D. Roosevelt for president.

Closer and closer! Finally, in the "'Round the County" news from Chokio in the February 7 issue of the *Morris Tribune,* I found the confirmation I needed: "Mrs. Mae Kirwin and Albert Reichmuth were in Mankato Saturday. Mr. Reichmuth represented Chokio at the Democratic convention."

And, I hoped, Mae Kirwin had met Mike Fritz. I was not sure if this was where they met; possibly they knew each other from some time before. But at least I had placed them in the same town at the same time.

Pat Conroy, who grew up in Chokio and is a good friend of my aunt Pat, remembered thinking that Mae's relationship with this Mr. Fritz was so wonderful and mysterious, because, as she put it, "everyone else was just married folk." She remembered Mae taking the train to meet Mr. Fritz in Minneapolis, so discreet.

☙

I drove to Mankato in late November to see if I could find what was left of Michael D. Fritz in the town. I was looking for three places: the last house he lived in—the address I had was 121 Clark, but I had heard that the street name had changed to East Pleasant; the two houses he had built on Oak Knoll; and Tincomville, the part of town where he had gardened.

First I drove up to his house on Pleasant. It was larger than I expected. He had shared it with only one other man— a Mr. Young—a two-and-a-half-story house with a wrap-around front porch. A fine example of the Queen Anne style, the house sat on two lots. There was evidence of a concrete foundation for a wrought-iron fence on the borders of the land.

Next, at Oak Knoll, I walked along the bottom of the slope that would have sheltered his tulips. It was a bright sunny day but the wind was pulling the last of the leaves off the trees. I wondered if anything was left of his gardens come spring.

At first, no one could tell me where Tincomville was, but then I read that it was near Stoltzman Road, the old Bohemian area of town. Looking at a map of Mankato, I saw that all Mr. Fritz's energies had been focused around a slough area surrounding Troost Pond, an older section of town.

I looked through an old history of Mankato and found a picture of the newspaper staff, purportedly from 1880. In this picture is a man identified as H. D. Fritz—not M. D.— but once again, I knew I had found my man. I recognized him from the other photos I had seen. Dark hair, full mustache, deep, dark eyes. A very handsome man. I think the picture was probably taken close to the time Mae was born.

If Mike Fritz asked Mae to marry him, I'm not surprised she turned him down. He was Presbyterian, he was Republican, and he was twenty-six years older than she. Also, she certainly would have had to quit her job, leave Chokio, and move to Mankato—a town where she had no history.

Aunt Pat says Mae said no to Mike Fritz because she didn't want to share her children with anyone. Somehow, this reason seems more of a children's explanation for why Mae wouldn't remarry. For whatever reason she turned Fritz down, it was probably just as well—for they wouldn't have been married long.

Mike Fritz fell and fractured his skull in the fall of 1940, about four and a half years after he met Mae. He never fully recovered from the injury. Then, in late April 1941, he suffered a heart attack and died in the hospital a few days later. The funeral services, according to his newspaper, were "attended by more than three hundred persons." He would have been seventy-three the next month. I'll always wonder if Mae knew about his death and if she sent a bouquet of flowers, maybe gladioli.

Recipes and War
1940-1960

But we who will eat the bread when we come in

Out of the cold and dark know it is a deeper mystery

That brings the bread to rise:

                it is the love and faith

Of large and lonely women, moving like floury clouds

In farmhouse kitchens, that rounds the loaves and the lives

Of those around them . . .

Thomas McGrath
"The Bread of this World"

Overleaf: Mae, mid-1940s

want to find the woman in the midst of her life. What I really want, have long hoped for, is that cache of letters that someone has saved, someone to whom my grandmother wrote often and intimately, or the diary in which she noted her closest thoughts and hopes. But I haven't discovered them and have just about given up hope of ever finding much in the way of written words from my grandmother.

It is easy for me to see the reasons why my grandmother left so little writing behind. She worked long days and didn't have much time for correspondence or journal writing. She never really left home; everyone she might have written to lived close around her. But, most importantly, I know that letters she wrote weren't saved. My family, for the most part, weren't hoarders. They traveled light. When I asked around to all my relatives for anything that my grandmother had written, what I received were recipes and one letter. The recipes often had someone else's name on them, like "Mrs. Olsen's meatballs." Ironic that a woman whose job it was to move letters between correspondents wrote so few herself.

⁓⟴⟿

The decade of the thirties was, for my grandmother as for much of America, a time of "hunkering down." She worked; she kept her household going and raised her children. She kept them close and nothing much happened to any of them, outside of mumps and a couple of broken limbs. She did travel some and she got out of the house to play bridge and socialize; she had a quiet, steady life.

This all changed in 1939, when my mother Ruthmary left home for college. It was the beginning of the exodus. For the next ten years, Mae Kirwin's children would swoop away from her and then settle in the nest for a time, only to leave again. The world also was unsettled and roiling about. Hitler ruled over Germany and was pushing at the borders. The Japanese were putting on a show of strength in the Pacific. America was simply watching all this turmoil as the decade opened but would not be allowed to keep its distance. Mae's children would be pulled into the world by this overwhelming war and one of them would be destroyed by it.

My mother always claimed she was the first person from Chokio, Minnesota, to graduate from college. I've heard nothing to the contrary and I've asked. Going to college was not a simple task for her. As Aunt Pat tells it, "In those years, very few children got to go on to school. Parents just didn't have the money. Well, it just wasn't the thing."

In order to earn money for college, Ruthmary worked in the post office with her mother for much of high school. She would fill in through the holiday rush. One memory she told me from that time was of chilblains on the back of her legs from the drafts in the post office. I didn't even know what chilblains were; she explained that after repeated exposure to cold, an area of the skin would swell and crack. The post office was heated with a wood stove. With the door swinging open all the time, it was hard to stay warm. And women had to wear dresses, which left their legs especially vulnerable to the cold.

In the fall of 1939, Ruthmary went off to college and worked serving meals at a boarding house for room and board. The second year, she came back home to Chokio because she had run out of money. She worked at the post office with her mother that whole year. She also went to high school at one o'clock every day and joined the geometry class to pick up a credit she needed for college. The class was for sophomores, so Dutt was taking it also. Pat had skipped the class in her sophomore year so she was in it too. For once, the three Kirwin girls were in the same class. According to Pat, Ruthmary got As, Dutt got Bs, and she got Cs.

Jim, Mae's second child, graduated from high school in 1940. By this time he had been dating Cecelia "Tead" Eisenmenger for several years; they would eventually marry. Tead lived in Graceville and attended St. Mary's Academy, the same Catholic high school Mae had graduated from. Tead met Jim when Chokio played the Graceville team in football. As she explained to me, "We were always going back and forth to the dances in the various towns." After high school, Jim stayed in Chokio and continued to work at the hardware store.

Because all of Mae's children were born within a little more than five years of each other, she must have known that after the first one left, the rest would follow quickly. But she probably didn't realize how far they would go and what extraordinary world events would take them away from the small town in which they grew up.

In spring of 1941, Pat graduated from high school and went to beauty school in Minneapolis. She stayed with the Ackermans—Lucille Ackerman was her father's sister—helped with the housework and baby-sat their four-year-old daughter in exchange for room and board.

By this time, the two younger children, Dutt and Billy, had become quite a handful for Mae. According to relatives, they hung around with a rough crowd, drinking and smoking. Since Mae wasn't home during the day, she couldn't "sit on them" about their behavior and they had no father to come down hard on them. Jim was working all day long and both Ruthmary and Pat were gone to Minneapolis, so Dutt and Bill had free rein of their lives.

Aunt Pat remembers one weekend when she decided to go back to Chokio with two friends of hers who were also going to school in the Cities. About nine o'clock that night, it was raining hard and they were only six miles from Chokio when they came over a hill to find two cars aimed at them, one trying to pass the other. It was either hit the passing car or take the ditch. Pat remembers, "Primmie took the ditch. . . . I had a gash across the top of my head and my back hurt. I didn't want to go home with all this blood streaming down on me. I went to this girlfriend's house and she washed me up and tied a kerchief over my head."

At ten-thirty, when Pat finally arrived home, Mae got up and told her that Dutt and Bill had been in a bad car accident the night before. They had been to a dance in Johnson, the next town to the west of Chokio, and Bill had had too much to drink. Dutt wanted to watch over Bill, so she went in the same car with him. They drove off a dead end. Dutt was still in the hospital, and Billy was home with stitches in his head.

According to Pat, "Dutt came home the next morning. She had a big cut on one arm and was a bit irrational. She had taken quite a bump on the head. Sometimes she'd be a little off-key with what was going on, but in a day or two she straightened out just fine. I don't know how mother survived those years."

With Ruthmary back at college, only three teenage children were home with Mae. Her hours at the post office continued to shorten. Tead moved to Chokio and worked for Mae in the post office. They started work at eight and as Tead learned more about running the place, Mae was free to leave by five o'clock.

Mae was forty-seven years old when the United States declared war on Japan in December 1941. Her husband had fought in World War I and now she would see her children fight in this war, which would become known as World War II.

The *Morris Tribune* for December 12, 1941, told the story for the people of Stevens County:

COUNTY HAS 197 MEN
IN NATION'S FORCES

Stevens county had a total of 197 young men in the armed forces of the nation at the start of the war with Japan this week, according to the records of O. A. Munroe, clerk of the county draft board.

Of this group 103 left here as members of the National Guard, most of them with Morris' own Battery B of the 217th CA (AA) whne that unit went to Camp Haan last February.

There are 18 Stevens county young men in the regular army of the United States. There are 24 more in the United States Navy, 4 in the United States [Army] Air Corps, and one in the United States Coast Guard.

An Associated Press map of the Pacific was displayed at the bottom of the page, with the headline: "War Flares In The Pacific." The caption underneath described what happened on December 7: "Japanese airplanes attacked United States defense bases in the Philippine Islands and Hawaii where 104 American soldiers were killed and three American ships were damaged." The last sentence explained that "this base map of the Pacific is for your use in spotting war developments."

Pictures of Pearl Harbor before the attack lined the page; beneath them a column featured the men and women from Morris who were known to be in the Pacific war zone. A chart compared U.S. and Japanese naval strength.

The other Morris paper, the *Morris Sun,* featured an article about a young man from Morris who was scheduled to reach the island of Guam with the navy on the day "the Japanese boast[ed] of having captured the island." Two young women with connections to Morris were living in Honolulu: "No word has been received from any of these young people by relatives here. About 12 to 14 days is required to get a letter from Hawaii and steamers have not been running with their usual regularity for several weeks, local relatives say."

But in other sections of the newspaper, life went on as usual in western Minnesota: in the *Tribune,* holiday hours for stores in Morris were listed, a talk on Grand Coulee Dam described, roll call funds for the Red Cross drive reported. The *Sun's* headline shouted, "SNOW ADDS TO HOLIDAY MOTIF."

The most telling item I found in either paper was in a *Tribune* story about a young man who wanted to get into the war so badly that he had asked permission to leave the United States Air Corps to join the Royal Canadian Air Force. When war was declared, his application for discharge was refused. The article opened: "Outbreak of war between the United States and Japan has changed the plans of many people." To say the least.

❧

The war sped up what was already happening in Mae's life—the exodus of her children. By 1942, four of Mae's children had moved away from home; by early 1943, all of them had left Chokio. Two went overseas.

Dutt did not graduate from high school in 1942. Instead she ran off with Joe Eisenmenger, Tead's older brother, that spring. Joe was eight years older than Dutt and was trying to make a go of it on the family farm outside of Graceville. They eloped to South Dakota to get married, not telling Mae. They planned it out in advance. The night before the elopement, Dutt told Pat and asked her to be the maid of honor. The wedding party of four drove right across the border to Sisseton, South Dakota. There they found a priest, but he would not marry them because he did not know them, their ages, or their religion. They asked him to call the priest back in Chokio, who okayed the marriage. But after some thought, the Sisseton priest still would not marry them, so they were married by the justice of the peace.

At two o'clock in the morning, they all arrived back in Chokio and woke up Mae to tell her. She was very upset. Jim came out of the bedroom, rubbing his eyes. To calm his mother down, he said, "It'd be a hell of a funny family if someone didn't get married."

But Mae still had trouble accepting the marriage. She felt that Joe was too old for Dutt and that Dutt was too young to know what she was doing. My mother told me that Mae even threatened to have the marriage annulled. A week after their elopement, Dutt and Joe were married again by the priest in Chokio. They went to live on Joe's family farm just outside of Graceville.

❦

In October 1942, Jim Kirwin and Clayton Virnig both left Chokio to serve in the U.S. Army. According to the *Chokio Review*, Jim "made somewhat of a record for promotions during his short period of training. On December 1st, just one month after his induction, he was promoted to the rank of corporal, and the first week of this month [February 1943] . . . he was promoted to sergeant." Jim was stationed at Camp Adair in Oregon.

Jim wrote back to the newspaper's editor, George L. Townsend:

Dear Geo.:

I want to thank you for sending me the paper each week. I find a lot of things of interest to me in it. I suppose Chokio is real peaceful without all of us young outlaws around anymore.

This army life really runs into work but we can't think of our own discomforts at a time like this.

Please say hello to all my friends for me and continue sending me your paper.

The pinch of the war began to be felt even in Chokio. In November 1942, coffee rationing began. The paper announced rationing would start at the "rate of 1 pound every 5 weeks for each person over 15 years of age starting at midnight of November 28th. . . . On the basis of 35 to 40 cups to the pound, the ration means slightly more than a cup a day per person." I imagine this changed the length of coffee breaks at the post office.

The post office became more than ever the communication pipeline into the community. The U.S. Post Office issued a plea on November 12 to shop and mail early:

The Post Office Department now is starting the most gigantic task in its history—the movement of a deluge of Christmas parcels, cards and letters while maintaining the regular flow of millions of pieces of mail daily to and from our armed forces all over the world. . . .

About 25,000 experienced postal workers have been taken by the war services. Arrangements are underway to add thousands of temporary personnel to postal staffs, but this man power is hard to find and is inexperienced. Facilities of railroads and air lines are heavily taxed by movements of huge quantities of war materials and personnel. Extra trucks are almost impossible to obtain. Winter weather, hampering transportation, is beginning.

The free mailing privilege granted to members of the

armed forces has raised their mailings some 30 percent, it is estimated. Expansion of those forces also is adding rapidly to the postal burden. . . .

The Post Office Department is making strenuous efforts to avoid such a terrific jam as it faced in 1918 under similar conditions, during the First World War. It can succeed in those efforts—and avoid many heartaches for its patrons—if the public will cooperate by mailing early.

Mae worked hard during the week. Most weekends, someone came to visit—often Dutt and Joe or Pat, who was now working in a beauty shop in Graceville, or Marguerite or Ruthmary might visit from the Cities.

On December 3, 1942, the *Chokio Review* reported that the War Production Board had asked city officials and citizens to dispense with outdoor decorative lighting for Christmas. Most of Mae's children were home for Christmas that year. Ruthmary came home from school, Pat came from Graceville, Dutt and Joe spent some time with Mae, and Bill was still living at home. However, the Christmas of 1942 was the first Christmas someone from the family was missing— Jim stayed on base in Oregon.

In May 1943, an announcement for a navy recruiter appeared in the Chokio paper. Billy was only seventeen years old, but if Mae signed for him, he could join up. She gave her permission, and in late August, Billy left home for the first time:

> Billy Kirwin left Tuesday for Farragut. Billy Kirwin, son of Mrs. Mae Kirwin of Chokio, left Tuesday for Minneapolis, from where he will be sent to Farragut, Idaho, where he will receive specialized training in the U.S. Navy. Billy recently enlisted when the navy recruiters visited Morris.

Pat joined the WAVES in the fall of 1943. As she explained, "Working at a beauty shop in Glenwood wasn't doing much to help the war effort." Because women under twenty-one needed their parents' permission, she, too, had to ask her mother.

On November 26, 1943, Jim returned home from the service and he and Tead married. Their good news was a welcome relief from the stories of the war. The *Chokio Review* gave their wedding a big write-up on the front page, describing, among other things, the bride's outfit:

> For the wedding, the bride wore a powder blue wool dress with brown accessories. Her bouquet consisted of yellow and white chrysanthemums and red roses.

Bill Kirwin on the USS Colorado, *about 1944*

No mention was made of what the groom was wearing, but I know because I have their wedding picture. Jim had on his uniform and looked handsome in it. I was surprised to see that the wedding took place at eight o'clock in the morning. At nine, Mae had a wedding breakfast at her home for the bridal couple and about twenty guests. Aunt Pat explained the early hour: "Eight o'clock was when mass was, so that's when they got married."

Theirs was the only marriage of which Mae completely approved. Jim and Tead were both twenty-one, old enough to know what they were doing. Mae knew Tead quite well and liked her. Most important of all, Tead was Catholic.

$\propto$

I have lost Mae. Amid the goings-on of all her children, I can no longer seem to find her. At the end of her time raising children she truly became a mother—there solely for her children as they circled her, then spun out farther and farther from home. The newspapers tell me where her children went, what they were doing, but Mae herself was no longer mentioned except when her children came to visit her. By staying in one place and doing what she had always done, Mae became invisible.

I did find one small notice of her on the front page of the *Chokio Review,* August 26, 1943:

KIDS TAMPERING WITH MAILBOXES

It has been brought to the attention of the post office department that there have been some instances of tampering with rural mail boxes and the mail contained therein. It is thought that this is the work of children, who go to their own mail boxes and where more than one box is located at the same place, have opened the other boxes and tampered with the contents.

Mrs. Mae Kirwin, local postmaster says, "If you send children after mail under such circumstances, be sure and

There are strange ways of serving
God.
You sweep a room or lift a rod,
And suddenly to your surprise
you hear the whir of Seraphim
And find your under Gods own
eyes, and building palaces
For him.

A favorite poem, or prayer, in Mae's handwriting

warn them that they may be involved in serious difficulties if any one else's box is opened."

The news of the war, however, overshadowed all other news. Young men were being slaughtered. Where once all a mother had to worry about was a farm accident, now every week some young man was killed—maybe a friend, a relative, the kid next door. In reading through the Morris papers, I was amazed to see that on the front page of every weekly paper there were usually two to three stories of local young men killed in the war.

A story in the *Morris Sun* showed how people in these small towns in Minnesota felt about their boys leaving home for the war:

There is this difference between America and Germany. In Germany the young boy is trained and educated to believe that to become a soldier is the greatest thing in the world. To march and handle weapons and to fight is most honorable. That is what makes a real man.

In America every boy is released by the home for the army with heartache and sorrow. When the army starts out from home, it is the hope of every one that the boys may soon come again. To us war is a scourge. It is "hell" as Sherman said. To Germany it means honor and dignity and fighting is the only thing that makes a real man.

Worrying about her two sons must have kept Mae occupied. She had reason to worry, as evidenced by the *Morris Tribune,* October 27, 1944:

Chokio townspeople are following the invasion of the Philippines with great interest because two of her favorite sons, S/Sgt. Clayton Virnig, son of Mr. and Mrs. Henry Virnig, and Pvt. Jimmy Kirwin, son of Mrs. Mae Kirwin, are members of the 96th Infantry Division which landed on the island of Leyte last week. Mrs. Kirwin has another son, Wm. Hugh Kirwin, F1/c, who is with the Navy in the South Pacific.

Jim was wounded nine days into the Battle of Leyte. He wrote his mother from the hospital in New Guinea and described his time fighting with his division on Leyte:

D plus 7 we were still moving abreast the road. The 2nd batalion was having quite a time taking the town of Tabontabon so we had to hold up a little. We then went through the town behind them. It sure was a sight, dead horses, dead Japs and burning buildings. The smell was terrible, we could hardly stand it.

D p[l]us 9 this was the last day for me, we kept advancing all day up both sides of the road. Dug in about five that night. Captured our first Jap prisoner today (alive if you can believe that). Just after dark the Japs counter-attacked and we opened up with everything we had. Ten minutes later we received another attack there was plenty of fireworks. I could see the bullets throw the mud up in front of my hole.

Just then my leg began to sting and burn. I felt of it and looked at my hand, it was all bloody. My buddy in the foxhole yelled over "We have a man hit over here." In a few minutes a medical man had fixed me up. The battle was over for me. They took me out of my foxhole and carried me back to Bn. Aid. I layed back there on a stretcher all night. The next morning I was loaded on a jeep and taken to the evacuation hospital, here they gave me more morphine then a local and cleaned my wound, bandaged it and marked me for evacuation. I was evacuated on D plus 11 to a ship and taken to a general hospital from where I am writing this letter. As I left the beach I was half glad and half mad, the battle was over for me.

⟡

Thinking over Mae's life during the forties, I realized that the one person who was around her the most while all her children were gone, involved in the war effort, was Tead Eisenmenger Kirwin. Tead now lives in Grand Rapids, Minnesota, and, at the end of the long Thanksgiving weekend in 1994, I called her to ask her about life in Chokio during the war years. I figured she would be home after spending the holiday with her children.

Tead told me that after she had married Jim, she moved in with Mae for a while in 1943 and worked in the post office with her. Like Selma Gillies, the hired girl, she said that Mae Kirwin was easy to work for, "good natured and even tempered."

Soon into our conversation, she told me that she would never forget the day when they came to tell Mae that her youngest son Bill had been killed in the war. The news was delivered by telegram. It came to the train depot and Spencer Klucas, the depot agent, received it. He walked over to the bank and got Albert Reichmuth, Mae's brother-in-law, who worked there as a bookkeeper. Tead said Albert was a "prince of a man." The two men walked into the restaurant to find Tead. She always took her morning coffee there after the mail was out. The two men told her what had happened to Bill and what they had to do.

They asked Tead to go back to the post office and act as if nothing had happened. Tead remembered walking into the back of the post office and seeing Mae sitting there at her desk, working. The two men came in and told Mae that her son was dead. Then they took her over to the Red Owl to get her sister-in-law, Jean Kirwin. Jean stayed with Mae back at her house.

The worst had happened. Mae had lost one of her children, the youngest, the one born after her husband had died, her baby. William Hugh Kirwin, his father's namesake, died at the Battle of the Philippines in Leyte Gulf on November 27, 1944. Mae saved a postcard of his ship, the USS *Colorado*. Where the address should have been Billy had simply written the word *Mother*.

Telegram, 1944

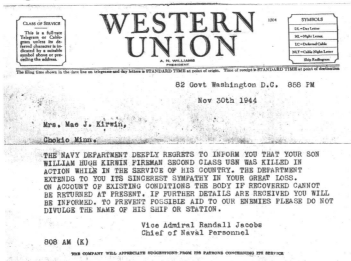

WESTERN UNION

CLASS OF SERVICE
This is a full-rate Telegram or Cablegram unless its deferred character is indicated by a suitable symbol above or preceding the address.

1204

SYMBOLS
DL = Day Letter
NL = Night Letter
LC = Deferred Cable
NLT = Cable Night Letter
Ship Radiogram

A. N. WILLIAMS
PRESIDENT

The filing time shown in the date line on telegrams and day letters is STANDARD TIME at point of origin. Time of receipt is STANDARD TIME at point of destination

82 Govt Washington D.C.   858 PM

Nov 30th 1944

Mrs. Mae J. Kirwin,

Chokio Minn.

THE NAVY DEPARTMENT DEEPLY REGRETS TO INFORM YOU THAT YOUR SON WILLIAM HUGH KIRWIN FIREMAN SECOND CLASS USN WAS KILLED IN ACTION WHILE IN THE SERVICE OF HIS COUNTRY. THE DEPARTMENT EXTENDS TO YOU ITS SINCEREST SYMPATHY IN YOUR GREAT LOSS. ON ACCOUNT OF EXISTING CONDITIONS THE BODY IF RECOVERED CANNOT BE RETURNED AT PRESENT. IF FURTHER DETAILS ARE RECEIVED YOU WILL BE INFORMED. TO PREVENT POSSIBLE AID TO OUR ENEMIES PLEASE DO NOT DIVULGE THE NAME OF HIS SHIP OR STATION.

Vice Admiral Randall Jacobs
Chief of Naval Personnel

808 AM (K)

THE COMPANY WILL APPRECIATE SUGGESTIONS FROM ITS PATRONS CONCERNING ITS SERVICE

Within twenty-four hours, Ruthmary, Marguerite, and Pat had joined Mae in Chokio. Ruthmary and Marguerite came up from the Twin Cities, and Pat flew in from Norfolk, Virginia, after her commanding officer stayed up all night making sure she had priority to fly all the way through to Minneapolis.

Pat had not learned of Bill's death from her mother. She had been working at Norfolk, correcting code books for the navy, when she heard the first bad news. Jim had been wounded in action in the same battle, going in on foot with the army. Bill was in the backup seaguard. Pat had asked for any additional information, so when the Red Cross called and told her to come over to their office, she assumed they had something to tell her about Jim:

> One of the girls in our office went over with me and when I got there they sat me down and asked me family things. And finally they said, what about your younger brother, your brother Bill? Right then I knew something was wrong, because I hadn't told them I had a younger brother, I hadn't told them anything. So that's the way it was.

The whole town of Chokio mourned the death of Bill Kirwin. The *Chokio Review* reported, "Mere words cannot express the shock and deep sorrow that spread over the community on Friday of last week when Mrs. Mae Kirwin received a telegram from the war department, stating that her youngest son, William H. Kirwin, F 1/c, had been killed in action aboard ship in the Pacific." All the businesses in town planned to close for the memorial service at St. Mary's church.

Pat told me that Mae took his death just terribly. She had very bitter feelings about other young men his age who had not enlisted in the armed services when he had, in particular a nephew that had been Billy's same age. But Mae never once regretted that Billy had gone to war.

I have a photograph of Bill on the ship. He leans over the white-chain guard rail, dressed in his uniform with a dark navy hat sitting slightly tipped on his head. Bill had a smile that would break any woman's heart. I remember as a child sitting and staring at that picture, thinking that he was so handsome, wondering what he would have looked like if he were still alive.

In the photographs that have passed down in the family, there is a snapshot of the memorial service held on the *Colorado* on December 3, 1944, for the men killed in the action. A dark photograph: in the far left corner, a minister preaches behind a cross. An armed color guard stands at attention on the side of the ship. Most of the frame is filled with the bowed heads of men listening to the service. The horizon stretches across the top of the picture. Other ships dot the ocean. A large white wave hits the side of the ship.

Bill died exactly fifty years before I called Tead Kirwin to ask about his death. She reminded me of that fact as we talked. I hadn't noticed when he had died; I didn't realize that I was calling on the anniversary of his death. She told me then that Bill had died a year and a day after she and Jim had married. Bill was eighteen years old when he was killed by the Japanese.

❦

I heard about the kamikaze pilots when I was a kid, probably playing a war game with the boys. It was a fun word to say, *kamikaze,* but it was not until I was in my teens and studying World War II, which seemed to me to have happened in another century, that I came to know what the word meant.

When I was born in 1952, the war had been over for only seven years, so it must have been still fresh in my parents' minds. I do not remember either of them ever talking about it much. The only comparable war I've experienced, albeit not first hand, is the Vietnam War, which has been over for twenty some years. That war still feels very much a part of my life, which helps me imagine how my parents thought of World War II.

At my birth, Billy Kirwin had only been dead for eight years. When I was researching Billy's death, I came to a new awareness of World War II and of how the word *kamikaze* came to be.

World War II is amazingly well-documented—the military made use of all the current technology to capture what was happening to their troops. As a result, incredibly detailed books have been written on the war, using numerous photographs and film clips to show the fighting.

In looking through *The American Heritage Picture History of World War II,* I read about the enormous battle in which Billy died: "In the last days of October [1944], some 70 Japanese warships and 716 planes, split into three separate commands, opposed 166 American warships and 1,280 planes in the greatest naval battle of all time, the Battle for Leyte Gulf." This battle was when the kamikaze, or suicide, pilots first attacked. The strategy of the kamikaze pilots, devised by Vice Admiral Takijiro Ohnishi, was simple. Since the Japanese had no planes to waste, they needed every one of them to count as much as possible. The fighters were armed with 550-pound bombs and their pilots were told to crash onto the carrier decks. In Japanese, kamikaze means "divine wind," referring to a typhoon that blew away a Mongol fleet set on invading Japan. The pilots who flew these kamikaze missions were young, in their early twenties, and saw their assignments as an honor. Their anthologized farewell letters to their families give a painfully clear view of their feelings. One man wrote on the last page of his diary: "Like cherry blossoms / In the spring / Let us fall / Clean and radiant."

And fall they did. When I wanted more specific information, I found the fifteen-volume *History of United States Naval Operations in World War II.* In volume twelve, *Leyte June 1944–January 1945,* I looked for the day Billy died, November 27, 1944, and found the subhead: "2. Kamikazes in Leyte Gulf, 16–29 November."

Billy's battleship, the *Colorado,* was still stationed in the Leyte Gulf along with 3 other battleships, a heavy cruiser, 4 light cruisers, and 16 destroyers. On the morning of November 27, the fleet was standing by to fuel up when it was attacked by 25–30 enemy planes. Two of these planes headed for the *Colorado:* "one struck the port side amidships and the other splashed close aboard." The kamikaze plane that hit the ship must have been the one that killed my uncle.

I previously used the analogy of a wind sweeping through my grandmother's life to take my grandfather out of it because tornadoes are such a part of life on the prairies. Here was a second wind—the Japanese "divine wind"—and it blew the second man out of my grandmother's life. Bill was a fireman on the ship and was working below deck when the battleship was hit. He was killed instantly. The crew sealed off that section so that it wouldn't fill up with water and sink the entire ship.

By the end of the Battle of Leyte Gulf, the Japanese had lost 56,263 men, the Americans only 2,888. The Philippines were wide open to the Allies, and Japan was left quite unprotected, although the war in the Pacific would go on for almost another year.

In early 1945, Jim Kirwin left the hospital in New Guinea and rejoined his division on Leyte. After he arrived back, Jim met a soldier who told him he had been one of the crew who helped remove bodies from the *Colorado* and that he knew where Bill's gravesite was. Jim was granted a leave to go find the gravesite. He wrote his mother and said he would send her a complete report on the location and services for her younger son.

⚓

The war ended twice in Chokio, and each time the town knew what to do. As the war in Europe was wrapping up, Mayor A. G. Moffatt reminded the residents of Chokio of the rules adopted by the village council:

1. Stores will close.
2. Churches will open and arrange appropriate services.
3. Liquor store will close.
4. No beer will be sold.

After President Harry S. Truman announced Germany's defeat at eight o'clock on Tuesday morning, May 8, 1945, the Chokio fire siren blasted for five minutes, joined by the ringing of all the church bells in the town. According to the *Chokio Review,* "quiet thankfulness was prevalent throughout the village. Churches held services during the day and evening with large crowds attending. Many with mixed feelings of thankfulness and concern for a war still to be won in the Pacific."

Three months later, on August 14, the siren blew a second time to announce the news of Japan's surrender. In the post office, Mae took care of all the mail deliveries and then shut down for the federal two-day holiday. She probably went to church and then home to drink a beer and cry for the son who would be coming home and for the one who wouldn't. Again, the *Chokio Review* recorded the atmosphere in town: "There were not many people on the street or in town and as a whole the day was quiet with people giving mute testimony of their thankfulness to the end of a terrible war."

The scenes of jubilation and craziness in the big cities

are how I think of the war's end. I didn't realize the reaction would be so different in a small town. There were too many losses, too much sorrow, for any kind of celebration to go on.

On February 11, 1946, Mae received a military award and a Purple Heart for her son Billy. Because he had died in the war, she became a Gold Star mother.

⟶

Mae's children started coming home: Jim went on furlough and never had to report back to his division; Pat came from Yorktown, Virginia; and Ruthmary from St. Louis, where she had been working for the Red Cross. The *Chokio Review* announced in June 1946 that 786 men and women, about 74 percent of Stevens County's service people, had mustered out.

Teadie and Jim settled into the old Reichmuth house, which they bought from Mae's sister Edna. Tead told me that one day Edna came over and criticized the flowers she had planted out front. Teadie was young and tender, and when Jim came home she was crying. He asked her what was the matter, and when she told him, he said, "Edna got her money. We can plant whatever we want to plant."

Pat and Ruthmary stayed with Mae. They decided they wanted to paint her house. She wouldn't let them paint the outside, said it was too big a job for the two of them, so she hired a man to do that. But they painted the whole inside. Pat described this time:

> We sang and we painted and we painted and we sang. By the time the first of June came we had the house all redone. All these kids were coming out of the service and everyone was doing work for their parents on all the houses that had gone defunct during the war. Everyone would go downtown with all their paint clothes on and have coffee or a can of beer until five, five-thirty, dinner time.

Soon after this, Ruthmary moved back to Minneapolis and took a job working at Wonderall, a local company that made coveralls for small children. Pat stayed on in Chokio. One night she went to a dance and caught the eye of a dapper young man. He found out who she was from a friend and called a few days later to ask her out. Al Anfinson had not gone into the service because he had been crushed by a horse and had lost his senses of taste and smell. He was working at a filling station in Morris. Pat married Al less than two months later on June 6, 1946.

This was another marriage Mae wasn't very happy about. Al was not Catholic, but at least Pat was married in the church by a priest.

> I was marrying a non-Catholic and my mother was very upset. She didn't do anything but pout around for I don't know how many weeks. Then she got real sick four days before the wedding. Doctor gave her some . . . medication. We were up with her twenty-four hours and all this goings-on. She was a little bit better. Finally it was the day before we were going to get married. I said to her, "Mother, if you think you aren't going to be well enough to get up and go to the church, then I'll talk to the priest and we'll be married in your bedroom." That did it. She thought she could stop us from being married at that time until she could talk to us, or I don't know what her thinking was. She didn't want me to get married and leave home. I was twenty-three years old. So when I told her we'd get married in her bedroom, she got up that evening for a while and then the next day we got her dressed and she went with us.

The couple was married in a double ring ceremony at the church by the Reverend Father M. Billmayr. Ruthmary was the maid of honor. A dinner for the immediate family was held at Jim and Tead's house. Fourteen people attended, including Al's mother and father from Benson, Minnesota. For their wedding trip, the couple toured northern Minnesota.

In 1943, Mae became a grandmother. She was nearly fifty, none too young to move into this new role. On September 22, James Patrick Eisenmenger, Dutt and Joe's first child, was born in Graceville. Mae was in attendance when the baby was born as she would be for most of her grandchildren.

As the oldest grandchild, Jimmy Jo knew Mae quite well. He can remember sitting out on her front steps on Sunday morning and reading the paper. "All the women in the kitchen cooking fried chicken on Sunday."

The second grandchild, Mary Jo, was born in 1945, another Eisenmenger. Mary Jo spent a lot of time at Mae's in the summer, eating rhubarb from her garden patch near the alley. She remembered Grandma charging up her electric golf cart and driving it into town two blocks away to do her grocery shopping. Mary Jo told me that Mae used White Rain shampoo to wash her hair and Deep Magic moisturizing lotion to remove her makeup.

The third grandchild, Kathy Kirwin, was born in 1946 to Tead and Jim in Chokio. She knew the town quite well; her family lived there off and on until she was nine years old. Like all the other grandchildren, she had fond memories of Mae's hollyhocks alongside the house.

The fourth grandchild, Hugh Anfinson, was born to Pat and Al in 1947 in Chokio. Hugh spent a lot of time with Mae. She often went and picked him up from school while his parents were both working at the cafe. He told me how he burnt his nose on a cookie sheet when he was smelling the cookies. He remembered Mae smoking and reading all the time. "*Reader's Digest,*" he said. "She always had the *Reader's Digest.*"

Ultimately, Mae had eighteen grandchildren. All but one

of them were born in her lifetime. Doris Margaret Logue, Ruthmary's youngest daughter and my sister, was born in 1962, a year after Mae died.

❦

In the midst of all these births, another death occurred. Marguerite, Mae's wonderfully flamboyant younger sister, had been living in Minneapolis and drinking quite heavily. The stories about her drinking abound. Mae let it be known that she did not want her drinking when she came home to visit in Chokio.

However, at Ruthmary's college graduation in Minneapolis, Marguerite created a scene. "Aunt Mickie," as she was known to her nephews and nieces, had quite a "little bit under her belt" that day, according to Pat. Ruthmary's graduation was such an important event that many relatives came down from Chokio. Mae and Edna and Dutt were all there. Pat told the story: "As I heard it, they got to this big auditorium [probably Northrop]. Marguerite was cracking wise and she had a mayonnaise jar or peanut butter jar with whiskey in it in her purse, and she kept having a little to keep her going. I guess it must have been raining. They had umbrellas. Finally, one woman made some remark about the noise Aunt Marguerite was making or whatever, and Aunt Marguerite turned around and hit her with her umbrella."

She was only forty-one when she died unexpectedly of cirrhosis of the liver. Mae was in the Cities, visiting Pat at the time. They brought Marguerite's body back to Chokio. She was buried in the Catholic cemetery there near her father. Of the nine children born in the Peter and Honora McNally family, only three remained by 1947—Mae and Edna in Chokio, and Irene, who still lived in the Fergus Falls institution.

❦

In 1946 Mae retired. She had worked for the post office about six years as assistant for her uncle Charles McAllen and her father Peter, and those years counted toward her retirement. With her own eighteen and a half years as postmaster, she had worked long enough to retire. She was through. Saturday, August 31, 1946, was her last day of work.

The *Chokio Review* reported ponderously: "No retirement is more justified than that accorded Mrs. Kirwin, she has had more than her share of life's hardships and has always cheerfully and courteously adminitsered the duties of her responsible public position."

When I began work on this book, I ran across the article on her retirement and read it for clues about who my grandmother had been. I remember I was sitting on the porch at Joan McNally's house in Chokio, looking out across the field in her backyard. The clipping read, "Her plans for the future are indefinite, but [she] jokingly stated she would like to write a book on the many interesting experiences during her long term of serving the public."

❧

On March 9, 1948, some Chokio women formed the American Legion Auxiliary of Chokio Post No. 629. According to an auxiliary legion history, "The weather was very cold and a small group of women, 16 in all, attended." Two women from an auxiliary in Willmar came to present the aims and purposes of the organization and to help set up this unit. Dues were to be two dollars a year. "A few members of the Legion served a delicious lunch." Mae Kirwin, a Gold Star mother, was elected president that day. Because she was now retired, she could become active in civic and social organizations.

I had known that Mae was in the auxiliary but hadn't

realized she was its first president. When I was in Chokio for a visit, Kay Grossman and I decided to go into the Legion Hall and see if we could find any information on the auxiliary for my book. We borrowed the key from the woman who runs the grocery store across the street. The Legion is housed in a long, narrow building that faces Main Street. The small front room is filled with a handsome wooden bar that I remembered from when my mother's high school class celebrated its fiftieth reunion.

We stumbled through the next room and had trouble finding lights to turn on to see. In the very back room we found a four-drawer metal file cabinet. The second drawer contained the history of the auxiliary. The Legion auxiliary always appointed historians to keep track of what they did and who exactly did it.

The auxiliary was a spin-off of the veterans' group, the American Legion, which was formed in Paris after World War I in March 1919. The first U.S. caucus was held in St. Louis two months later and the first convention was held that fall in Minneapolis.

Theodore Roosevelt, Jr., an early organizer of the Legion, spoke at its St. Louis caucus:

> We will be facing troublous times in the coming years and to my mind no greater safeguard could be devised than those soldiers, sailors, and marines formed in their own association, in such manner that they could make themselves felt for law and order, decent living and thinking, and truer "nationalism."

In 1919, the American Legion Auxiliary was established at the First National Convention of the American Legion in Minneapolis. Those eligible included:

> The mothers, wives, sisters and daughters of members of The American Legion, and . . . the mothers, wives, sisters and daughters of all men and women who were in the mil-

itary and naval service of the United States between April 6, 1917 and November 11, 1918, and died in line of duty, or after honorable discharge; and . . . those women who of their own right are eligible to membership in The American Legion.

Eligibility later expanded to include those who had served in World War II. Mae was eligible five times over: she was the sister of Hugh and the wife of Bill, both of whom had served in World War I, and the mother of three children enlisted in World War II.

Chokio's American Legion post held its first meeting on September 16, 1947, and the auxiliary formed six months later. I hope that the relationship between these two organizations was respectful and cooperative; there had been some resistance in the Legion nationally when the auxiliary was first formed. Counsel General James Drain of the national Legion mentioned it in his speech to the auxiliary at their convention in Miami in 1934:

> I remember the apprehension with which some of the men looked upon the creation of the Auxiliary. I remember some of the men thought we were just inviting trouble—to get a lot of women in the thing and "then what the heck will we do?" I will tell you what we have done.
>
> There has not been . . . a single serious case of misunderstanding between The American Legion and its Auxiliary since the Auxiliary was created. Your little pledge in your Handbook . . . has, almost without a single exception, been lived up to to a degree which could only be explained on one hypothesis: you women do know things without knowing how you know them; that is, you know you can trust us, blundering as we are, to, in the end, do the right thing.

I was delighted to find the preamble of the Chokio auxiliary, since I assume it follows the format of the "little pledge" to which Drain referred. This preamble is full of the language that comes when a country and a people are trying

Ruthmary Kirwin pointing to names of her relatives who served in World War II, late 1940s

to regroup and are strongly defining themselves as united:

> For God and Country we associate ourselves together for the following purposes:
>
> To uphold and defend the Constitution of the United States of America, to maintain law and order; to foster and perpetuate a one hundred percent Americanism; to pre-

serve the memories and incidents of our association during the Great Wars, to inculcate to the Community, State, and Nation; to combat the autocracy of both the classes and the Masses, to make right the master of might, to promote peace and good will on earth; to safeguard and transmit to posterity the principles of justice, freedom and democracy; to participate in and to contribute to the accomplishment of the aims and purposes of the American Legion; to consecrate and sanctify our association by our devotion to mutual helpfulness.

The Chokio auxiliary adopted resolutions, many of which had to do with how to handle the deaths of its members, for example: "Upon death in family of a unit member, the Memorial Committee will send card of condolence," "Upon death of Unit member or member of immediate family, the Memorial Committee shall go to the home and offer assistance," and "Upon death of a paid-up Unit member, the Auxiliary members shall attend the funeral in a body." The final resolution stated that an auxiliary grave marker would be purchased and installed for each auxiliary member. When Mae Kirwin died in 1961, an auxiliary marker was placed on her grave.

A general meeting of the newly formed auxiliary was called less than a month after its founding and sixty members attended. At the May 3 meeting, the officers were installed during a ceremony that was described as "short and impressive." President Mae Kirwin received a gavel. Mrs. James (Tead) Kirwin gave a report on the committee meeting for Memorial Day. The auxiliary decided to march as a group in the parade and that the Gold Star mothers would ride in a car.

The slogan of the auxiliary was "Service—Not Self." In its first full year, the members sewed clothes and other items for the veterans' hospital. They collected fifty pounds of rags to be shipped to the federal veterans' hospital at St. Cloud for the veterans to use in making rugs. They helped with the March of Dimes, Sister Kenny, and cancer drives. The Americanism Committee prepared a bulletin of facts about the flag and distributed them to the Chokio public school and to all the surrounding rural schools. They held a poppy poster contest and awarded prizes. The unit also sent a girl to Girls State in the summer.

The historian, Mrs. A. G. Moffatt, from whom Mae had bought her house, summarized their first year: "THUS— things which no government can do, things that require the touch of personal interest and human understanding, the Chokio Auxiliary thru its 90 members is doing."

Mae Kirwin's reign as president of the auxiliary was short because the organization was formed in March. On June 7, 1948, the nominating committee reported the new nominees, who were then unanimously elected. Mrs. Mae Kirwin talked about the district convention to be held at Glenwood the next week. For entertainment, the Girl Scouts under the direction of Mrs. Clayton Virnig performed their flag ceremony and read the history of the Girl Scouts, then sang "America" and "Taps." According to the minutes, "This was very interesting and enjoyed by all."

Mae Kirwin went to the convention at Glenwood and later gave a short report on it and announced the state convention to be held in Minneapolis in August. At the August meeting, the new president asked for delegates to the state convention, and Mrs. Mae Kirwin offered to go.

At the September meeting, the past president Mrs. Mae Kirwin installed the new officers. The group appointed an official pianist for the next year. The new president announced that no cookies were to be sent to the veterans' hospital for fear of the polio patients there.

Mae remained active in the auxiliary for the rest of her life.

In 1950, two of Mae's children, Pat and Jim, along with their spouses, Al and Tead, bought a dude ranch in the wild west. Al had seen an ad for it in the Minneapolis paper and he and Jim went out to take a look at the ranch. They liked it and decided to buy it.

Camp Sawtooth was located in Wyoming, at the top of a pass that loops south between Red Lodge and Cooke City, Montana. It was reachable only on horseback, a ride of four miles from the pack station. The first year, the two families and Mae went out to Red Lodge and waited for the high road into the park to open. Then Jim and Al went in to set up the camp while the others stayed behind at the station.

I have a picture of Mae wearing a broad cowboy hat and a plaid jacket, seated astride a horse, a split rail fence behind her and huge pine trees surrounding her. She looks easy on top of a horse and happy with the adventure of it all. My

Mae at the dude ranch, Camp Sawtooth, Wyoming, about 1950

mother, Ruthmary, rode in the first year to help out. The whole family pitched in, but the dude ranch was a doomed venture.

Pat explained: "It was quite a thing—all of us dummies going into the ranch knowing nothing about it whatsoever. We really, really worked. We had the ranch for three years, during the Korean War crisis. During that time, nobody was traveling because of the war scare, and reservations were cancelled. It was a bummer. The old boy that we bought the ranch from had sold it several times before and gotten it back. That was his policy—get their down payment and freeze them out. He tried like everything, but we hung on for three years and finally decided it was no good for us, so the third year we folded up and left for good."

Finally, in 1950, Mae's twenty-nine-year-old oldest daughter Ruthmary married an accountant she had met at Wonderall. The thirty-two-year-old ex-Marine sergeant was from southern Minnesota and had gone to the University of Minnesota as a music major. He changed his major to business and passed his CPA board exam in Chicago.

Ruthmary Kirwin married Robert Pershing Logue on the "Sweetest Day" of the year, October 20. It was a great disappointment to Mae when Ruthmary chose to marry out of the church. Although my father's father, Frank Logue, was an Irish Catholic, his mother, Louise Oestreich, was a German Lutheran. Her religion prevailed and so did my father's. Ruthmary considered not marrying Robert because he was Lutheran, but in the end, she renounced her faith.

Because the priest at Chokio threatened to excommunicate Mae if she went to a wedding in a Lutheran church, my parents' wedding took place in Dode and Jim MacRae's house in Minneapolis. A Lutheran minister officiated. My diminutive mother, five foot one inch tall and (maybe) ninety pounds, wore a full-length white wedding dress of Chantilly lace with a seed pearl neckline. She cut off the long train and fashioned it into a mantilla so she would look taller standing next to my six-foot-two-inch father. Dutt was the matron of honor, dressed in pale blue silk. Pat and Al also attended. Louise Logue, the groom's mother, wore a gray dress, with a corsage of yellow mums. Mae attended the wedding dressed in black.

⟶⟶

Mae kept busy after she retired. I can't imagine her ever sitting still, unless she had a book in her hands or was sewing on something. Aunt Pat said that the first thing Mae did after she retired was to sew three layettes for her new grandchildren: Kathy Kirwin, John Eisenmenger, and Hugh Anfinson. Next, she attended to her house. She remodeled it, had the kitchen completely redone. Joanie McNally remembered talking with her about wallpapering or a new table she bought. One of her nieces remembered Mae getting very fussy about her house when she retired. "When she got a broom in her hand, watch out."

Mae's son Jim asked her to come and live with him. Mae said, "Jim, no way in hell. I've got my own life."

Mae did work around the house that she had never had time to do before. For the first time in her life, she was actually a homemaker. She mended clothes for herself and her neighbors. There was an empty lot between her house and the neighbors', and she often gardened on that land, putting up canned goods in the fall. She planted two big crabapple trees and made jelly from their fruit.

Despite their age difference—Joanie was in her thirties, Mae in her sixties—Joanie McNally and Mae Kirwin became quite good friends in the 1950s. Joanie and Bud were very good friends with Pat and Al. So when Pat and Al lived in Chokio, Mae was often at events with the four of them. When the Anfinsons left town to live in Grand Forks, Joanie recalled she invited Mae over for dinner.

Mae always made it a point to read the latest book to come out. Joanie and Mae both belonged to several book clubs and they passed books back and forth. Mae seemed to be trying to make up for lost time in retirement.

Joanie told me:

> We had the same interests such as reading and politics. We got to going back and forth very steady. At least once a week, Mae would come over to spend an evening, or I'd walk over there. It was never a short visit. It usually ran to well after midnight. So I'd walk home with her. Bud would usually go to bed about ten o'clock, he'd say, "Well, ladies, I'm going to bed. I've gotta work in the morning."

But as much as Mae seemed to belong in Chokio, she thought of living elsewhere after she retired. She went out to California to see if she might settle there, but nothing ever came of it.

❧

When I think of my grandmother, one thing I remember is that she traveled. I will never forget a black bar of Magno soap made by the Spanish cosmetic company La Toja that my mother kept tucked into her top drawer—a deep, rich, musky smell pervaded her handkerchiefs and jewelry. My grandmother had picked the soap up on one of her trips and it made me think she had been to Spain when actually I know now she had only been up to Canada.

In their later years, Mae and Edna got along better. Donna Reichmuth, Edna's daughter, remembered Mae stopping by to visit. She wouldn't take her coat off, saying she was only going to stay a minute, but she would end up staying an hour or two. Edna and Mae went to the movies together in Morris or Graceville. They even took a trip together, going to Mardi Gras in New Orleans with a tour group by bus. Mae later said they had ringside seats to everything and that she had a great time.

Mae often traveled with other friends. Jean and George Kirwin, her in-laws who owned the Red Owl in Chokio, moved out to Nevada after they retired. She traveled out west with them. Mae told the story of how she and George were sitting in a station waiting for a train. By this time, Mae had gone rather deaf, and George was blind. He would listen for the station announcements, and she would watch the clock. She said she turned to him and said, "We really need each other, don't we?"

Another friend she traveled with was Mary Doyle, who was about ten years younger than Mae. Mary was a fourth-grade teacher who had been a captain in the WACs during World War II. She and Mae would sit up and drink coffee and smoke half the night away. As two single women in a small town, they had that much in common. The two of them traveled up to Alaska together to see Dutt and Joe. At the time of her death, Mae was talking about going to Europe with Mary Doyle. It would have been her first trip abroad. I wonder if they were considering going to Ireland.

But most of Mae's traveling was going to visit her children. She spent most Christmases with Jim, although once or twice she was with my family. I've been told often of the Christmas I was three and Helen was one and I pulled the Christmas tree over on top of Helen. Mom said Helen looked so funny sitting on the living room floor in the midst of the tree with tinsel hanging off of her. She cried but wasn't hurt. My mother and Mae laughed and laughed and then rescued the baby.

Four generations, October 1952: Barbara Kirwin, 83 years old; Mae Kirwin, 58 years old; Ruthmary Logue, 31 years old; Mary Logue, 6 months old.

I have come back to the recipes, small bits of paper with my grandmother's writing on them. Sometimes they were written on note cards, other times just on scraps of paper that were convenient. What they mean to me is that someone ate something that my grandmother made and asked her for the recipe—they liked her food. For many women, recipes might be all the writing they ever did in their lives. For many women, the act of cooking food might be all they were ever known for. Not true of my grandmother Mae, yet it hit me hard that when I asked my relatives for any letters they received from her, all they could find were her recipes.

Mae wasn't particularly known for her cooking, and many of the recipes she gave to her children were ones she passed on from other women in the community. I have eighteen recipes in her handwriting, five of which she attributed to other people. Two of the women were given their married names—Mrs. Lee's Pumpkin Cake, Mrs. Conera's Salad Dressing—and two women were named more informally—Grandma Kirwin's Spice Cake (this would have been Mae's mother-in-law) and the ever-popular Betty Crocker's Children's Cookies. The final attribution was to a brand-name product, Skippy Cookies, telling me pretty clearly where the recipe came from.

Six of the recipes are for cookies, six for cakes, four for salad dressings and pickles, and two for main course meals. Now, this proportion makes some sense. Women tended to cook simply for main courses—meat and potatoes, boiled vegetables, food they were taught to cook by their mothers—who needed recipes for that? But when they brought treats to picnics, church dinners, bazaars, and luncheons, they often brought cakes and cookies; that is, baked goods.

Baking is more like a science, while cooking is more like an art. You need to be exact if you expect your cookies to come out the way they did last time, while you can put into a stew the vegetables you have available. Thus, women wrote down recipes for the foods they brought out into public, festive baked goods.

Two recipes existed in two slightly different versions—Bread and Butter Pickles and Old Fashioned Ginger Cookies—so I decided they must have been specialties of hers. I decided to bake the ginger cookies:

OLD FASHIONED GINGER COOKIES
¼ cup Soft Shortening
½ cup sugar
1–egg–½ cup Molasses
Place in large bowl, and mix thouroughly.
1 teaspoon of soda in ½ cup of hot water add to above
   mixture
2 cups of flour to which add

½ ts. salt--1 ts ginger ½ ts nutmeg
½ ts. cloves–½ ts Cinnamon
add to the liquid and mix
Chill dough, and drop by ts
on greased cookie sheet.
Icing
¾ cup powdered sugar. Add Vanilla and Cream to easy
   spreading consistency.
Orange juice may be used instead of Cream.

Like my mother, I don't bake very often, but I wanted to succeed with these cookies so they would at least be edible. I lined up all my ingredients on my kitchen table and went to work, thinking about what I had learned from my mother that must have been passed down from Mae.

Take mashed potatoes. Now, my mom passed on to me two hints about mashed potatoes that I think improve their quality immensely and that I know she learned from Mae. After she boiled up the boiling potatoes, she saved some of the potato water for the gravy, but she left about a half an inch of water in the bottom of the pan to begin to mash the potatoes in. Second, she heated up the milk on the stove before she added it to the potatoes, so they didn't cool off. Once the potatoes were mashed and steaming, she heaped them up in a large blue bowl and put a knob of butter on top to melt and a couple of shakes of paprika for color.

Back to the cookies. For starters, I want to point out what was not in the recipe. Women assumed much and wrote down only what they needed to in their recipes. Mae didn't tell us how long to chill the dough. She assumed that whoever she had passed her recipe on to would know how long to chill it until it was the right consistency to handle easily.

She did not write down how hot an oven to use or how long to bake the cookies. Most women knew that cookies took a medium-hot oven (325 to 375 degrees) and that they baked for ten to twelve minutes. The other reason this information was left out of the recipe is that ovens varied more than they do today. It made no sense to give information that wouldn't match up with all ranges.

I mixed up the batter and let it chill. While it was in the refrigerator, I stirred up the icing. I made two changes in Mae's recipe. Hers called for one teaspoon of ginger. We had no dried ginger in the house, so I substituted fresh. Fresh ginger would never have been found in a kitchen in Chokio in 1950, and it probably still would not be today. Mae's icing was to be made with cream. I used milk instead, and not just milk, but 2 percent, certainly something my grandmother would neither have had nor thought to use.

When the batter was stiff, I gouged it out of the mixing bowl with a teaspoon as directed and dropped it onto the cookie sheet, hence the term for this kind of cookie—drop cookies. I found that they baked well at 375 degrees in my oven for close to twelve minutes. When they had cooled, I drizzled icing on all three dozen of them.

Then I sat down and ate one. It was a solid, slightly spicy, rather cakey cookie. Not fancy, but tasty and substantial. Probably fairly close to what they tasted like when my grandmother made them. I thought of her kitchen with its south-facing windows. I saw her moving around in it with a gingham apron on, covering her flowered dress. She might have made me these cookies. I ate another one.

Away from Home
1960-1995

While my mind was scourging itself with trying

　To taste my mother's burial, whole, complete,

Through the white silence flew so gently

　A robin, without confusion, without fear.

She remained above the grave as if knowing

　That the reason for her coming was concealed to all

But the one who was waiting in the coffin

　And I was jealous of this intimate, strange talk.

The air of Heaven descended on that grave there,

　There was an awful, holy mirth about that robin,

I was cut off from the mystery like a novice,

　The grave was far away though I was beside the coffin.

Seán Ó Ríordáin
"My Mother's Burial"
Translated from the Irish by Gabriel Fitzmaurice

Overleaf: Mae, 1961

will always remember the day my grandmother Mae Kirwin died. I was nine and a half years old. We all have stories we carry with us, stories that define who we are, moments we will never forget. The late November day in 1961 my Grandma Kirwin died is one of those days for me. I wrote about the day in a short story called "Time to Be There."

My other grandmother, Grandma Logue, had come to visit for Thanksgiving, and Dad and I were driving her home. She lived south of St. Paul in Waseca, Minnesota, about a two-and-a-half-hour drive. Grandmother Louise Oestreich Logue was old, bordering on ancient. In her early eighties, she always seemed much older than Grandma Kirwin to me. A big woman, she spoke with a German accent, although she had lived in Minnesota all her life.

None of us said much on the drive down. When Dad drove into Waseca, he stopped off to see his cousin Rollie Malloy, my godfather. Rollie owned the flower shop in town. Dad only wanted to run in and say hello, so Grandma and I sat in the car. After a few minutes, she looked down at me and told me not to cry when she died, that it was getting close to her time. I nodded my head and then started to cry. She did, too. When Dad got back to the car, we wiped away our tears and said nothing about why we had been crying. He didn't ask.

When we got to Grandma's house, we all went in. She turned on the old gas heater that sat in the front room. I loved to watch the small flames of fire dance around inside the stove. I don't remember if we were going to stay for dinner. It didn't matter, because my mother called. My grandmother answered the phone, turning it upside down so that the speaker was near her hearing aid, which she wore pinned to the front of her dress. My mother's voice projected out into the room. She wanted to talk to my father.

They did not talk long. When my father got off the phone, he told me that my grandmother was dead. After a stunned moment, I realized who he was talking about: Mae Kirwin, my mother's mother, had died. We got back into the car. I sat next to my father all the ride home, and he never said a word to me. I was afraid I had done something wrong. I was too scared to ask him anything. We stopped to pick up his half-sister Ramah so she could watch us kids while Dad and Mom drove up to Chokio.

When we arrived home, a crowd of people filled our new house, which we had only moved into the previous week. I didn't see my mother. Then I was told that she was in her bedroom, lying down. When I peeked in the door, I saw her sprawled on her side of the bed, the side closest to the door. She was crying. She told me her mother had died in a car accident. She said it was not fair, her mom was only sixty-seven, too young to die. Dutt had been badly hurt, too.

My parents left the next day to go to Chokio for the funeral. I was the oldest, but even I didn't get to go to my grandmother's funeral. I had school and I needed to stay home and help Ramah watch the other children. I remembered the last time I had seen my grandmother Mae Kirwin: it was only a week or two before her death.

I have made much about not getting any correspondence of Mae's, but I actually did receive from Tead Kirwin a copy of one letter Mae wrote to Jim. It may have been the last letter Mae ever wrote. It was dated November 14, 1961, Chokio:

Dear All of you,—Dut and I got home at 11 P.M. last nite—and are we bushed— Got them all moved and it was really a deal. and besides every last one of us from Bob, right on down had the flu. Too much eat, drink, and staying up late.

You left your camera, tie, Barbasol and Old Spice lotion at Ruths. Jimmy Jo and I might be up for Christmas if you have no other plans. Dut will leave about the 8th or 15th and then we have some work to do, but will write you more in a week or so. We will bring your things if we come. No news from Pat sins she left. She's probably busy. Hope all are well. Love to all, Mom.

Not a long letter and certainly not very revealing, it was rather a quick note to convey a few pieces of information. Mae wrote it after she and all her children had been down in the Twin Cities, helping my family move.

My parents had bought a lot in the wilds of Lake Elmo, a suburb of St. Paul. While they were building a house on this land, they sold our house in Shoreview. In the interim, we had no place to live. A friend of my father's, Jack Kelly, let us live in his lumberyard.

Mae came down with Pat and Dutt to help us move into our new house, even though it was not completely finished. Pat recalled that she and Dutt were so "damned mad" at Mae because she had insisted on bringing a frozen turkey with them on the bus. Since everyone was gathered together, we had an early Thanksgiving celebration. I have several pictures of the whole crew of us gathered around the counter at the apartment we were staying in at the lumberyard. Casual photographs of a smiling clan, but no single shots of Mae.

The whole Mae Kirwin family was in these pictures: Dutt

One of the last photographs of Mae, Osseo, Minnesota, 1961.
Left to right: Dutt Eisenmenger, Mary Logue, Pat Anfinson,
Jamie Logue, Bob Logue, Ruthmary Logue, Helen Logue, Mae
Kirwin, Jim Kirwin, Robin Logue.

looked sideways at the camera, Aunt Pat had her arms
around me, my mom Ruthmary had her arm around my sister Helen, who leaned into Mae. Jim held the youngest
Logue, Robin, who was only two, in his lap. At sixty-seven,
Mae looked great. This was the last time I ever saw her. She
wore a polka-dot dress and her gray hair had a nice springy
wave to it.

❦

When my mom came home from Mae's funeral, I knew
from what she said that the accident had been a real tragedy,
that there was some question about who was responsible for
it, and that Dutt was having a hard time. In my family, no
one ever whispered around the children. My mother was
always pretty straightforward about what was going on, as
were my relatives.

What I pieced together from all the stories I've heard is this: Sunday, November 26, 1961, was the day before the seventeenth anniversary of Billy's death. Dutt had come home to Chokio from Alaska for a nice long visit. She was going back in mid-December. Dutt, Mae, Bud McNally, and Joanie McNally had a drink or two together at the bar in town. Dutt wanted to visit some friends near Graceville, and she asked Bud if she could borrow his car, a 1954 Ford station wagon. He handed her the keys.

Dutt and Mae drove off at a little before three in the afternoon. On their way to the friend's, they came to a country intersection. Typical of a rural road, it had no stop signs. Dan Lane of Graceville was out hunting pheasant from his car. He had his shotgun on the seat next to him, and he was watching the fields for any sign of movement.

The two cars approached each other, Lane heading east and Dutt going south, and collided in the intersection. Bud's station wagon flew into the ditch on the east side of the road, the door popped open, and Mae was thrown out, hitting her head. She died of a neck fracture and head injuries. The death certificate states that the interval between the accident and death was five minutes. Dutt hurt her pelvis. Dan Lane was uninjured. According to the *Graceville Enterprise,* "Damage was not considered extensive as the Lane car's grill was torn off and the other car was damaged only on the right rear side."

In reconstructing the accident from this information, I imagined that Lane entered the intersection after Dutt, clipped the back of Bud's wagon, and pushed it into the ditch on the east side of the road.

When I was out driving in the countryside around Chokio, I came to understand all too clearly how such an accident could occur. Rural roads are minimally maintained and dirt surfaced, with intersections every mile, and there is not much traffic, especially on Sunday afternoons.

Because I never saw other cars, I began to think I never would. My driving grew sloppy. I did not pay attention to the center of the road because it was not marked. I became almost unconscious of the fact that I was in a car. I didn't drive very fast: rather, I drifted along, paying a lot of attention to the scenery around me and not much to the road.

It is hard to ascribe fault in an accident like this, and most often no one tries. But in this case, Dan Lane decided to take Helen (Dutt) Eisenmenger and Joseph (Bud) McNally to court. Jim Kirwin, in the name of Mae Kirwin's estate, sued Dan Lane. He also sued Bud McNally, or rather, Bud McNally's insurance company. I could not determine who sued first.

❧

The civil trial to determine fault in the car accident of November 26, 1961, in Big Stone County that killed Mae Kirwin started in May 1962. In the *Ortonville Independent,* "A Constructive Newspaper in a Live Community," May 24, 1962, the spring term of the state Eighth District Court was front-page news. Chief Judge E. R. Selnes from Glenwood heard civil case number three:

> Dan C. Lane vs. Helen Eisenmenger and Joseph McNally. This involves an auto accident, in which the plaintiff, Lane, is asking judgment against each of the defendants in the amount of $547.20.

Further in the article was the seventh civil case:

> James P. Kirwin, as Trustee of the Estate of Mary J. Kirwin, decedent, vs. Daniel Lane and Joseph McNally. This is another auto accident case, and the plaintiff demands judgment in the amount of $25,000.

A week later the *Ortonville Independent* reported that the two cases had been consolidated for the purpose of the trial. Because the accident had happened in Big Stone County, it would be tried at the county courthouse. Dan Lane was well known in this county as a school board member and a lifetime member of the Gun Club and Golf Course. Lane's golf scores were reported in the Graceville paper while the trial went on. Mae, in contrast, had lived in Stevens County. Pat told me that the Kirwin family asked for a change of venue, but the judge would not allow it.

All Mae's surviving children attended the trial—Ruthmary, Jim, Pat, and Dutt. Dan Lane's attorney subpoenaed Dutt and flew her in from Alaska. The other Kirwin children were not happy about this; they felt that she had already been through enough. She still was not feeling at all well. To get Dutt into the courtroom, the family had to put her in a chair and then carry her up and down the steps of the courthouse.

The trial lasted a week and all the Kirwins went every day. Joanie and Bud McNally, although their insurance company was being sued by the Kirwin family, attended the trial in support of Mae's children. After all, Mae had been one of Joanie's best friends.

Joanie told me:

You'd think it would be long, a whole day in court, but it just . . . went so fast. . . . The trial was a whole week trial. Now, that was unusual for a car accident. They had my husband Bud [Joseph McNally] two days on the stand when the only time he had seen the accident scene was after the cars had been removed. They had him on the stand for two days because they were having a lot of fun with it. Neither lawyer could mix him up on the directions of the cars. He would say, "No, you're wrong." It got to be funny.

She had been to the scene of the accident and described to me what she had seen:

Our car was hit on the rear right fender. She [Dutt] was going from the north to the south and he was coming from the west. The car was hit on the rear fender which sprung the frame. From the outside the car didn't look bad, but was pretty damaged. Now, I think what happened was when Lane hit them, the door sprung open. How she got out of that car, I don't know. I still to this day can't see what happened. The force of Lane's car hitting them in the right rear fender pushed the car clear across the road and down into the ditch. Although, why that would do that I have no idea. Because you would think that hitting the back would make it go the other way. I never could figure that out. Then the car was sitting upright. Hit by such a powerful force.

As far as what Dutt said had happened, Joanie continued,

Dutt said she saw him coming. She said she did not realize . . . how fast he was going, you don't normally drive that fast in the country. She was probably going forty, forty-five. That's how fast you should go on a country road. You don't speed on a gravel road. You slide and slip and you're apt to lose control of the car. She saw him, but she didn't realize he was coming that quickly to the intersection. She thought she had plenty of time to get through it. Fact is, she was practically through it.

According to Joanie, on the last day of the trial, Dan Lane announced in court that he was going sixty-five miles an hour and wasn't paying attention.

I requested a copy of the verdict from the Eighth District Court. The verdict was all I could get. Because the case was a civil suit, none of the transcripts had been kept. The verdict read:

We, the Jury impaneled and sworn in the above-entitled action, answer the questions submitted to us by the court, as follows:

1. Was Helen Eisenmenger guilty of negligence which was a proximate cause of the accident? Yes.

2. Was Daniel Lane guilty of negligence which was a proximate cause of the accident? No.

3. The next of kin of Mary J. Kirwin have been damaged in the sum of $10,886.75 Dollars.

Arnold Wolner
Foreman

The jury's decision angered my family. Not only had Dutt been present when Mae died but she had also been declared responsible for her death. The other children didn't believe the accident was her fault. Joanie McNally thought the jury made the decision it did because all its members were State Farm–insured and so was Dan Lane, and they didn't want their insurance company paying the claim. Aunt Pat thought it was partly because Lane was so well known. She told me that he had been in a previous accident in which two people had died and that his attorney had told him that if he were found guilty in this accident, he would be sent to jail. Pat felt that Lane wasn't always completely truthful in describing what had happened when he hit the car Dutt was driving.

Although the family wasn't happy with the jury's decision, the court demanded a high payment for Mae's death and that felt good to them. Their worst fear had happened—their mother had died—but at least she had been found worth a high price, as much as would have been asked for any man.

The Kirwin children all stayed in Chokio during the trial. The *Chokio Review*'s "Brevities" noted that "Mrs. Al Anfinson [Pat] of Great Falls, Mont., and Mrs. Bob Logue [Ruthmary] of St. Paul were Wednesday visitors of Mrs. Floyd Spaulding" and that "The Jim Kirwin family of Grand Rapids has been spending last week and this week in Chokio, while attending the court session in Ortonville due to the death of his mother, Mae Kirwin, in an automobile accident."

There was no mention of Dutt being in town or of the outcome of the trial in either the Chokio or the Ortonville paper.

The court made an "Order of Distribution" of the allotted moneys:

> I. That said Trustee [Jim Kirwin] pay to the firm of Stahler and Giberson, Morris, Minnesota [their lawyers] the sum of Two Thousand Seven Hundred Seventy Two & 55/100 Dollars ($2,772.55) plus costs in the amount of Thirty-four & 55/100 dollars ($34.55).

> II. That said Trustee pay unto himself as Administrator of the Estate of Mary J. Kirwin, Deceased, the sum of Eight Hundred Eighty Six & 75/100 Dollars ($886.75) for the funeral bill of Mary J. Kirwin.

> III. That said Trustee pay unto himself the sum of One Thousand Five Hundred Seventy Five & 81/100 Dollars ($1,575.81). [The same amounts were to be given to Ruthmary and Pat] . . .

> VI. Further, it is hereby Ordered that upon filing of the cancelled checks showing payment of the above-entitled amounts as directed herein, said Trustee shall be discharged.

Because Dutt had been found negligent in the accident, she was not given any money in the settlement. However, the other children found a way around the court order: they split the settlement four ways instead of three and sent Dutt her share from the checks they received.

The money came from Bud McNally's insurance company. Dan Lane did not receive any money for his damages.

Jim was thorough in handling Mae's estate. On October 7, 1962, nearly a year after his mother's death, he sent my mother a final accounting, four pages showing the payments to and receipts from Mae Kirwin's estate. A few of the bills he paid were $43.27 to Montgomery Ward, $71.00 to Dayton's, $9.91 for Western Union telegrams, $15.00 to Father Francis Hohn for the funeral mass, $15.00 to Wayne's Ambulance Service, $5.00 to Ruthmary Logue for house cleaning, and $20.00 to himself for expenses.

Mae died with $1,205.49 in the bank. From the sale of her house, her children realized $5,500.00. The total of her estate after expenses was $5,194.88. Her children split this four ways as they had done with the settlement.

Jim's letter to my mother:

Dear Sis:

Thank you for your check for Duts share. I will be sending her part to her very soon now. Enclosed is a check for $1,575.82 your share of distribution. Also a photographic copy of courts order of distribution. This is the last money we all will receive now. And with this act I have completed my work for you girls and for myself so if you have any questions please let me know because I want all you girls to be satisfied. I also want to thank you for your kind remarks in your letters. I enjoyed taking care of things for you girls as there is little or anything I can do for any of you anymore.

I received a long letter from Dutty today I forwarded to Pat and told her to send it to you. She's still having a tuff time.

Ruth you asked us to come down but everyone around here has been involved maybe some week end later you can bet we will come when we can. Maybe you would feel better a little later anyway. Not too much new around here Ruth. Kathy had her 16th birthday and of course Tead had a party for her 25 girls were here but everything back to normal again. Well Ruth write when you have time.

Love
Jim

I called my cousin Jim Eisenmenger to ask him what he remembered about the accident and the trial. He was eighteen years old when Mae died and he was down in Chokio with her and Dutt at the time. He remembered little. At that age, he told me, you don't pay attention to anyone but yourself. I reminded him that he had parachuted the day before in Graceville, hoping that might jog his memory.

Oh, he remembered that incident all right: "I thought I was going to die. I was supposed to land on the airstrip in Graceville but my main parachute malfunctioned and a piece of flotation gear didn't work. I was falling right toward Lake Toqua and the ice was so thin, I was sure I was going to go through. I started to take off my helmet which probably saved me. Taking off my helmet caused me to tip sideways and so I landed on my side, not feet first. If I would have landed feet first, I would have plunged right through the ice. As it was, my parachute pulled me across the ice, I could hear the ice cracking beneath me as I went."

Then, on January 15, 1962, Jim joined the Air Force, so he wasn't in Chokio for the trial.

⟞⟝

Wondering what had happened to Dan Lane, I looked him up on the CD-ROM version of the Social Security Death Benefit Record at the Minnesota History Center to find the date he died. The Graceville newspaper was no longer being published by then, so I read through the *Ortonville Independent* issues for December 1982 until I found his obituary.

Dan Lane was seventy when he died, which meant he had been forty-nine when his car struck the car carrying my grandmother. He had been a farmer for many years just outside of Graceville. He was a lifetime member of the Catholic church in town. The obituary did not mention the cause of his death. I was relieved he was dead, for I might have been tempted to call him up. What would I have asked him—what he remembered of that day? What he had been thinking of when he ran into the station wagon? What he thought of the court's decision? What he believed had happened?

⋙

When I think of Mae, I see parts of her that capture who she was. Most of all, I recall her hair. I knew her for nine years and her hair changed during that time, but I remember it as a blunt cut helmet of iron, an object with the ability to cut through the air and protect her head. And yet in the end it didn't. Her head folded, her hair covered with her blood.

I find myself searching for the truth in writing this book as if it will tell me something. Such a search can sometimes serve as a way of avoiding pain. It matters little how my grandmother came to die, whose fault it was, what actually happened in those few moments when car slammed into car—that she died when I was nine and not old enough to know her well is in the end all that has really affected me. The fact that she died as young as she did may well be why I have written this book. A truth.

⋙

Writing the end to a book like this is hard. I need to watch that it doesn't turn maudlin when, in the last few pages, I write of the trials and tribulations of my extended family, tell of the illnesses and deaths. In a novel, I can leave the reader in midair, soaring along with the main characters in full flight in the midst of their lives, but in a memoir, I must try to wrap up all the actual stories and show how Mae's children's lives played out.

None of Mae's four children stayed in Chokio. My mother

177

lived the rest of her life in a suburb of St. Paul, in the house my father and she built. At forty-two, she had her first heart attack—part of the Kirwin legacy. At fifty-six, she had triple bypass surgery; at sixty-five, she had a stroke; and she died at age sixty-six. She was preceded in death, as they say in the obituaries, by two of her children—Jamie and Helen. Her remaining three daughters, myself included, live in Minneapolis. I am the writer, the rememberer in the family, carrying on the stories. My sister Robin, in her mid-thirties, is studying pharmacy and Dodie is a sculptor. The three of us talk every day.

Jim, the second of Mae's kids, moved up to the Iron Range to Grand Rapids, Minnesota, where he worked for a mining company and then for a hardware store. He had five children. At fifty-seven, Jim had a heart attack at a hockey game and died a few days later. Again, the Kirwin Curse struck. His children are all alive; two still live in Grand Rapids near Tead. The three others live down near the Twin Cities and are married with children.

Dutt lived in Alaska for nearly ten years and then she left Joe. She moved down to Great Falls to be near Pat and worked in a fabric store for many years. I remember my mother going out to visit and coming back with bolts of fabric that would "make a great skirt." I inherited much of this fabric when my mother died. Dutt had a cerebral accident after having carotid artery surgery. She can no longer talk and doesn't have much use of her arms. But she communicates. Dutt is now living near her daughter Roni in Helena.

Last Christmas she wanted to buy Pat a specific present. When Roni couldn't understand what it was, Dutt dragged her outside, down the block, and pointed finally at the object—a large parasol clothes line for Pat's side yard. Roni bought Dutt such a clothes line to give to Pat.

Dutt's children live in Chicago, Sioux Falls, Alaska, and Montana.

Pat is Mae's only healthy child left. She divorced Al in her fifties but remained in Great Falls, Montana. Her three boys are scattered: Hugh lives in Burnsville, Minnesota; Bruce in Helena, Montana; and Scott in a small town north of Great Falls. She is painfully aware of being the last talker of the Kirwin family.

All in all, Mae's children had a total of eighteen children. Mae was very proud of these grandchildren and even had a special photo album for them, green with golden lettering on it proclaiming "My Grandchildren." I found it in my parents' room when we were cleaning out the house. At the beginning of the album, the pictures were ordered from oldest to youngest, but as more children came, the order was lost. Even some pictures of Mae's own children slipped in—Pat and Al on horseback, Uncle Jim looking like the Marlboro man.

Mae's grandchildren have produced twenty-three children of their own so far. They range in age from three to twenty-two.

Although Mae never made it to Ireland, her daughters each went there at least twice. Ruthmary was the first to go. When she was in her fifties, she and my father flew over to Shannon and traveled around, golfing and shopping. Ruthmary found some small plates with the name *Kirwan* on them, another spelling of her maiden name, and brought them back for her siblings.

The most extraordinary trip to Ireland was when the three daughters went over together. They talked about it for years afterwards. The three leprechauns, they called themselves—not one of them stood over five foot two in heels. They rented a car and drove around the island, snapping photos of each other and laughing so hard they had to pull over to the side of the road to pee. Mom took a picture of Dutt in the bathtub, another of Pat squatting in the weeds alongside the road, many of them in restaurants eating. Every night they went out to a pub.

My mother told me that one night, they decided they were too tired to go out. They were staying in a small bed-and-breakfast in the village of Killeshandra, in a home that usually boarded fishermen. The woman of the house was so glad to have three American women staying with them that she and her husband insisted on taking them out for a drink. Of course, they went. And once in the pubs, they sang. They sang all the Irish songs they had grown up with: "Danny Boy," "When Irish Eyes Are Smiling," and the like.

I have often wondered if my mother sang one of the songs I remember her singing to me as we hung up the wash in the backyard by the pond. I don't know the name of it, but the lines I remember are these:

> I've got rings on my fingers, and bells on my toes,
> elephants to carry you, my little Irish rose.
> So come to your Nabob on next St. Patrick's Day.
> Be Mistress Mambo Jambo Jijaboo Jay, O'Shay.
> Be Mistress Mambo Jambo Jijaboo Jay, O'Shay.

⟡

Years later, the trip to Ireland was repeated but considerably enlarged. The three original members—Pat, Dutt, and Ruthmary—took three of their own daughters—Roni, Dodie, myself—and their sister-in-law Tead. Jim Eisenmenger joined the crew in Dublin and traveled around for several days with us. We rented a van, and Roni, Dodie, and I took turns driving. The back of the van was the smoking section, where all the aunties sat, laughing and singing and screaming out "Whoa" if we drove too fast.

Every night we went out to a pub to hear music. We

drove back to Killeshandra and stayed with the couple there, but the husband was not in good health. On a rainy night we made our way into town only to find that a music festival was going on and the pubs were crowded with folk from the surrounding area. Music would break out from a group sitting in the middle of the crowd, a grandfather playing the fiddle, his granddaughter playing the tin whistle. At one point, a man playing the *bodhran,* a small hand drum, passed it to me, and I accompanied a couple of songs, pounding my way through the best I could.

We drank Guinness, we told stories, we laughed, we sang; in general, we carried on. But most important for me, we fit in. I knew these people: I had grown up with them. So many nights I had leaned an elbow on the counter of our kitchen at home and listened to my relatives tell stories and howl with laughter, asking for an old one that was an all-time favorite. We lived on stories, we relished them. So it was easy for me to talk fast and steady and keep up with the best of them. My sister Dodie and I both had shoulder-length, curly hair that we wore down that night; as we traveled from bar to bar, we were called the "girls with the hair." Rumors floated around town that we were from France or some other exotic place.

I kept a notebook on that trip and wrote a poem about the night we spent in that small Irish village:

Song in Killeshandra

Toward the end they ask Seamus to sing.
An old man lifts a wee girl
to his knee and gives her a taste of
foamy Guiness. The rain teems
through the night. We are safe.

Seamus lifts the shoulders of his shirt,
runs a finger down his thin nose and then,

like a wren, throws his head back and begins
to sing the song that we all know,
the words little changed, of loss and love

and loss and luck and we hope so much and get
so little. Something settles on us as we
breathe in the smoke-plumed air.
His voice flies in circles
and we watch as the bird batters his wings.

If only a window would open, the sky
would break, releasing his voice of trills
and valleys. Seamus sings the song
that our mothers taught us and our fathers
hummed coming home in the dark.

This trip helped me understand why I was a writer, why
words were as important as any food or drink to nourish life
in my Irish-American family. This trip was also the last time
that Mae's three daughters were together and healthy. That
fall, Dutt had her surgery and never fully recovered from
it. Two months later, my mother had her stroke. Within a
year and a half, she died, but not before asking me to write
a book about her mother.

EPILOGUE

The wind is what I will remember of this last trip. The whole time I was in Chokio, the wind didn't stop blowing. If I tried to walk down the street, a gust would coat my eyes and teeth with grit. At night the wind filled my dreams with grass swaying, trees bending. I heard the sound of it moving across the prairie all night long.

My grandmother Mae reminds me of the wind. Over the last two years, I have gathered so much evidence to prove that she was in the world and to show how she moved through it, but I feel as if she has slipped away from me. I hear her voice, I know some of her words, but the essence of her no longer exists in a place that once held her.

I don't mean to be melodramatic in calling this my last trip to Chokio, for certainly I will go back again, at least for the town centennial in 1998. And I am sure that, on a whim, I will get in my car and drive those two and a half hours northwest because I want to wander streets at night with Kay and talk about how the world looks from this western edge of Minnesota or listen to Joanie tell stories of my family.

But for a sense of closure to the story of my grandmother's life, I wanted to go back and see if I could find any last fact that I needed to put in my book. I called the lawyer who had worked on the civil trial when Mae died in the car accident. He was still living but did not remember the case. He suggested that I check in his old law office, which is still in

Morris. I stopped by the office, but they told me politely that they had "purged their files" twice in the last ten years. Needless to say, they found nothing left of the case.

Driving from Morris to Chokio, I knew it was time to quit, to stop following any more slight threads through old fabric. I took a deep breath and decided just to enjoy my trip back. All I would do is take a few pictures of what were for me historic landmarks, sit at the kitchen table with Kay, family, and friends, and drink cups of coffee and gab.

Which I did. But I also studied the town to see what was left of Mae. As I walked by her old house, I noticed that her crabapple trees were gone, that no hollyhocks were coming up on the south side of the house, but that the lilac bushes by the back door had popped open with lovely lavender blooms. The post office has moved, her house has new metal siding, her electric car is long gone. None of her children

Mae's house with hollyhocks, about 1950

lives in Chokio, but one of her grandchildren still strolls through the streets, taking notes.

I feel there is as much left of Mae in Chokio as there should be: scant evidence of her passing, a tip of the head to her place on earth, and then we walk on.

I am so glad I wrote the prologue to this book—my childhood memories of Mae—before I started my research. My sense of her has changed so dramatically that I would now be unable to write that prologue. I do not claim to understand my grandmother or even to know her much better, but I have acquired enormous love and admiration for her. She lived through the death of her siblings and her mother, she married and survived the death of her husband, and she made a home in which her children did not just grow but flourished. My mother, her oldest child, went on to the University of Minnesota and graduated from it thirty years before I did.

I am now able to picture Mae toward the end of her life, after her retirement. I know her well enough to do this. She sits in the front porch of her house, reading. She faces west, past the edge of town. A beer is within reach, a pack of cigarettes close by. The book she reads engages her, but from time to time she raises her head to note the progress of the sun. The prairie wind blows through the trees on the street, a sound she is so accustomed to that it barely nuzzles her ear.

She holds the book in her hand and thinks again, *I should write down my life. It would be worth it.* She thinks about the gang coming home for Sunday dinner, the chicken she has ready in the fridge. She rubs the bridge of her nose where her glasses rest. She reads until the light fades from the sky, late in summer, past ten, then finishes her beer. Maybe she sits in the gloaming and smokes one last cigarette. Then she stands up, runs her hands down her housedress, and goes in to bed. This is the way I will remember her.

EIGHT STEPS TO RESEARCHING A FAMILY HISTORY

There came a time in my life when I wanted to know more about my ancestors. It corresponded with reaching what I, at forty, saw as the middle of my life—an appropriate place at which to stop and look backward. Most people will feel this impulse at some time during their lives: the desire to know where they came from.

It is easy to want to write a family history, but where does one start? Because I am a mystery writer, I chose to view the process as a series of mysteries to be solved. Even if I didn't solve any of them to my own satisfaction, what I learned in trying was astonishing.

After the long and occasionally difficult process of writing my grandmother's history, I have come up with a series of suggestions I wish someone had handed me.

1. Begin with your living family. Like most endeavors, researching family history should start close to home. Ask your family to record their memories for you, or go and interview them. Find family photographs and documents. Get photocopies from relatives. Organize your material.

2. Gather your memories. Think back to your extended family's gatherings: reunions, parties, weddings, funerals, holidays. Write down the stories you have heard at these. What basis do they have in truth? You may be surprised. Let me give you an example.

My Irish-American mother, who had black hair, often told

me that we had some Spanish blood in our family. She said that Spaniards had visited Ireland and mixed their blood with ours. In the fall of 1995, I attended a conference in Minneapolis on Celtic spirituality. One of the speakers mentioned that the Spanish Armada had been shipwrecked on the coast of Ireland near Sligo. Several thousand Spaniards came ashore and mingled their genes with the Irish. Sitting in the audience, I felt an odd frisson of connection: could this have been the origin of my mother's tale?

3. Go back to the beginning. Visit the communities from which your family came. Walk down the streets, look at the houses, listen to the way people talk. History is hidden everywhere. All communities have repositories from which information can be gleaned: churches, schools, libraries, newspaper offices, banks, American Legion halls.

4. Read books. Immerse yourself in the past. Even if you don't use much of this information, the knowledge will fill out your story. I don't regret a moment of the reading I did around the edges of Mae Kirwin's life.

For example, some of the books I read helped me construct a framework for this story. One of the most helpful pieces was a short essay by Carolyn G. Heilbrun, "Dorothy L. Sayers: Biography Between the Lines." (I also highly recommend two of Heilbrun's books: *Writing a Woman's Life* and *Reinventing Womanhood.*) Her essay helped me see Mae Kirwin not as a victim of circumstances—her husband's death, the Depression—but as a strong woman who made tough choices. Mae's husband's death made it necessary for her to take a job, but I think she liked it. Mae had always worked: before marrying Bill Kirwin, she worked in the post office; after marriage, she ran a café with Bill in Winnebago. Even if her husband had lived, she might have chosen to work most of her life.

5. Be curious. Find out more than you need to know. When you stumble across an odd fact while researching

something else, track it down. I learned many things I couldn't fit into this book. As I was reading the early *Chokio Times*, I noticed how often stories mentioned the fact that people rode bicycles from town to town to visit each other. I had no idea that bicycles were so popular in western Minnesota at the turn of the century. Then *Minnesota History* published an article by Ron Spreng on "The 1890s Bicycling Craze in the Red River Valley," and it all fell into place.

6. Be thorough. Read all around the information you are looking for. I found this was particularly important of newspapers: even their ads offered clues to the lives I was studying. Take notes on everything. Nothing is more frustrating than to realize that a bit of information was important after all but that you can't track it down.

7. Be fierce. Don't give up when it looks as if the information is not available. When I couldn't find a record of Minnesota Democratic party conventions, I worked hard to figure out how else to locate the information. When I decided that to do so meant reading several years' worth of the Mankato newspapers, I went ahead and read them. It paid off.

Don't ever assume that an institution or organization will not give you information. Always ask for it, and if that doesn't work, insist. When I discovered that Mae's sister Irene McNally had been at the Fergus Falls Treatment Center, I called there immediately. If I had waited another few years, her records would have been destroyed, and I would never have known who my great-aunt Irene was. I had to work hard to find her, but it was worth it.

8. Have a quest. Make it more specific than simply finding out your family history. I gave myself several quests. Quests are good: they keep us moving when otherwise we might stop. The three questions I started with were: How did my grandfather die? Who was my grandmother's boyfriend? What happened in the car accident that killed my grandmother?

If you decide to research your family history, no matter how you go about it or what end product results, you will know more about yourself when you are finished. The world will seem a more interconnected place; historical events will take on new meaning as you begin to see them through your ancestors' eyes.

NOTES

Claiming Chokio

6   Epigraph: *Collected Poems of W. B. Yeats,* 31.

10   *Wall Street Journal* predicted: Charlier and Wall, "Life on the Land," *Wall Street Journal,* November 16, 1984, p. 1.

11   map of Stevens County: Andreas, *Illustrated Historical Atlas,* 180.

13–14   Chokio exists: Busch, *History of Stevens Co.,* 5–6, 30.

14   A small trading post: Busch, *History of Stevens Co.,* 184.

14   "According to my Dad": Dorweiler, *Chokio Community History,* 1–2.

15   railroad came to Morris: Busch, *History of Stevens Co.,* 6, 115, 184; Dorweiler, *Chokio Community History,* 2; Prosser, *Rails to the North Star,* 158, 160.

15   *Postmasters:* Patera and Gallagher, *Post Offices of Minnesota,* 178, 274; Jane F. Smith, Office of Civil Archives, National Archives and Records Service, General Services Administration, to James F. McNally, June 18, 1965, family papers.

15   John McNally, Sr., . . . petitioned: Busch, *History of Stevens Co.,* 111.

18   "The American Irish made it": Greeley, *That Most Distressful Nation,* 126.

19   *Potato facts:* Grubb, *The Potato,* 177–81, 512–14; Wyman, *Immigrants in the Valley,* 23.

21   one parish lost: Wyman, *Immigrants in the Valley,* 25.

21   "the direct stroke": O'Neill, "The Organisation and Administration of Relief, 1845–52," in *The Great*

Famine, edited by Edwards and Wilson (New York: New York University Press, 1957), 257.

21 money . . . spent on famine relief: Candaele and Candaele, "Revisionists and the Writing of Irish History," *Irish America,* July-August 1994.

21 Individuals were given: Wyman, *Immigrants in the Valley,* 29–30.

22 In the ship's records: Glazier, *Famine Immigrants* 4:173, 200.

22 John Nallen received his citizenship: Transcription of John Nallen's U.S. citizenship document, December 9, 1854, in notebook of McNally family history compiled by Kathleen McNally Eacho, hereafter family papers.

23 The first child born: Grace [McNally Christensen] to Ruth[mary Kirwin Logue], January 31, 1973, family papers.

23 "They came into the West": Shannon, *Catholic Colonization on the Western Frontier,* 102.

26 "from infirmities of old age": *Morris Tribune,* March 27, 1909, p. 5.

26 "Prosperous Pioneer Farmers": *Morris Sun,* August 22, 1918, p. 1.

28 "undaunted courage and unflagging industry": *Graceville Enterprise,* March 27, 1908, p. 1.

29 "So passes another pioneer": *Graceville Enterprise,* September 25, 1925, p. 1.

30 yet another plat map: *Standard Atlas of Stevens County, Minnesota,* 41.

Scrolling through the Family

34 Epigram: in *Eire-Ireland* 25 (Winter 1990): 19.

38 about 150 people living in Chokio: *Morris Tribune,* January 13, 1897, p. 8.

39 "chief-push at the Times office,": *Chokio Times,* April 7, 1897, p. 8.

42 six elevators operating: *Chokio Review,* July 5, 1973, p. 14B.

43 "Farmer's Elevator. A meeting is Called": *Chokio Times,* April 27, 1898, p. 4.

43 "Farmer's Elevator. A assured thing": *Chokio Times,* May 11, 1898, p. 4.

44 next meeting went well: *Chokio Times,* May 25, 1898, p. 4.

44 Today, Chokio has four grain elevators: *Chokio Review,* July 5, 1973, p. 14B.

45 "This reminds us of the Irishman": *Chokio Times,* July 13, 1898, p. 1.

51 family went to Morris: *Republican Times,* September 28, 1898, p. 8.

52 "a thriving little village": *Morris Tribune,* January 13, 1897, p. 8.

53 "Mrs. McNally Dies": *Morris Tribune,* March 17, 1916, p. 2.

54 Hugh, the oldest child: *Morris Tribune,* March 5, 1937, p. 6.

55–66 *Information on Irene:* Medical record for Irene McNally, Fergus Falls Regional Treatment Center, Fergus Falls.

71 Marguerite's obituary: *Chokio Review,* March 7, 194[7], p. 1.

72–73 *Information on St. Mary's Academy: Northern Star* (Clinton), June 22, 1978, Centennial Issue, part 2, "Graceville through 100 Years" supplement, 11; Wulff, *Big Stone County History,* 44.

75 Bill "left Morris": *Morris Tribune,* February 19, 1926, p. 1.

77 "one of Chokio's most charming": *Chokio Review* quoted in *Morris Tribune,* June 4, 1920, p. 1.

In and Out of the Depression

80 Epigraph: in Alzina Stone Dale, ed., *Dorothy L. Sayers,* 2.

82 Bill Kirwin's death: Death certificate for James W. Kirwin, which gives February 15 as day of death; *Blue Earth Post,* February 23, 1926, p. 1; *Winnebago City Press-News,* February 20, 1926, p. 1.

83 "caused by a misunderstanding": *Blue Earth Post,* February 16, 1926, p. 5.

84 "—The Swea City Herald notes": *Blue Earth Post,* February 23, 1926, p. 1.

84 "working with an electrical crew": *Morris Sun,* February 18, 1926, p. 1.

86 military funeral: *Morris Tribune,* February 19, 1926, p. 1.

87 His birth at the Morris hospital: *Morris Tribune,* March 19, 1926, p. 3.

89–90 *Information on postal appointments and pay:* Entries for Chokio, Stevens County, Minn., in U.S., Post Office Dept., "Record of Appointment of Postmasters, Minnesota, 1832–1971"; Langland, ed., *National Almanac and Year-Book for 1926,* 288, 295.

93 "There were no trucks": Alm, "Neither Rain, nor Sleet, nor Snow," in *An Honest Day's Work,* 104–5.

95 Grain prices had dropped off: Tweton, *Depression,* 9.

96 "Counties in west-central Minnesota": Tweton, *Depression,* 13.

96 "Dust storms are like that": Hudson, *Reapers of the Dust: A Prairie Chronicle,* 3.

101 *Information on St. Mary's church:* Dorweiler, *Chokio Community History,* 91–92, 93.

102 "Unquestionably, the parish priest": Greeley, *That Most Distressful Nation,* 85.

105 "other Minnesota postmasters": *Bronson Budget,* October 11, 1932, p. 1.

109 the *Bronson Budget* featured a big article: *Bronson Budget,* June 20, 1935, p. 1, 2.

112 a big anniversary jubilee edition: *Mankato Free Press,* fiftieth anniversary edition, April 5, 1937, Free Press Section, 3.

113 The *Mankato Free Press* . . . was very Republican: Lundin, *At the Bend in the River,* 117.

113 "Mr. Fritz has always voted": Hughes, *History of Blue Earth County,* 404–5.

113 "His extensive gladioli garden": *Mankato Free Press,* March 1, 1941, p. 1, 6.

114 "There was the mark of the creative artist": *Mankato Free Press,* March 3, 1941, p. 5.

115 The Democratic party: Blegen, *Minnesota,* 477, 478; Auerbach, *Worthy to Be Remembered,* 9–12, 15–17, 29.

118 an old history of Mankato: Lundin, *At the Bend in the River,* 117.

119 Mike Fritz fell: *Mankato Free Press,* March 1, p. 1, 6, March 4, p. 9, both 1941.

122   Epigraph: in *The Bread of this World; Praises III*

129   Jim Kirwin and Clayton Virnig both left Chokio: *Chokio Review,* August 16, 1945, p. 1.

129   "made somewhat of a record": *Chokio Review,* February 18, 1943, p. 1.

130   "Dear Geo.": *Chokio Review,* March 18, 1943, p. 1.

130   "rate of 1 pound every 5 weeks": *Chokio Review,* November 5, 1942, p. 1.

130   "The Post Office Department now is starting": *Chokio Review,* November 12, 1942, p. 1.

131   an anouncement for a navy recruiter: *Chokio Review,* May 6, 1943, p. 1.

131   "Bill Kirwin left": *Chokio Review,* September 2, 1943, p. 1.

132   "For the wedding": *Chokio Review,* December 2, 1943, p. 1.

134   "There is this difference": *Morris Sun,* March 24, 1944, p. 6.

135   Jim was wounded: *Morris Sun,* December 8, 1944, p. 1.

135   "D plus 7 we were still moving": *Chokio Review,* December 13, 1944, p. 1.

138   "Mere words cannot express": *Chokio Review* quoted in *Morris Tribune,* December 8, 1944, p. 1.

140   "In the last days of October": McCullough, ed., *American Heritage Picture History of World War II*, 532–33.

140   "one struck the port side": Morison, *History of United States Naval Operations in World War II,* 12:366.

141   Jim Kirwin left the hospital: *Chokio Review,* March 8, 1945, p. 1.

142   "Stores will close": *Chokio Review,* May 3, 1945, p. 1.

142   "quiet thankfulness was prevalent": *Chokio Review,* May 10, 1945, p. 1.

142   "There were not many people on the street": *Chokio Review,* August 16, 1945, p. 1.

143   On February 11th, 1946: *Chokio Review,* February 14, 1946, p. 1.

143   The *Chokio Review* announced: *Chokio Review,* June 13, 1946, p. 1.

147 In 1946 Mae retired: Smith to McNally, family papers; Chokio entries, in U.S., Post Office Dept., "Record of Appointment."

147 "No retirement is more justified": *Chokio Review,* August 22, 1946, p. 1.

147–152 *Information on the American Legion Auxiliary:* Records, American Legion Auxiliary, Chokio Post 629, Chokio; Moley, *The American Legion Story,* 50–63, 85; Thompson, comp., *History,* 33–34, 36, 45; Adams, *American Legion Auxiliary,* 3–4, 163–64; *Chokio Review,* September 18, 1947, p. 1.

Away from Home

165 Epigraph: in Declan Kiberd and Gabriel Fitzmaurice, eds., *An Crann Faoi Bhláth,* 49.

165 a short story: "Time to Be There," *Minnesota Monthly,* November 1985, p. 46–47.

169 "Damage was not considered extensive": *Graceville Enterprise,* November 28, 1961, p. 1.

171 Dan Lane was well known: *Ortonville Independent,* December 29, 1982, Section 1, p. 6; *Graceville Enterprise,* May 22, 1962, p. 3.

172 "We, the Jury": Verdict, May 29, 1962, *James P. Kirwin, as Trustee of the Estate of Mary J. Kirwin, Decedent, v Daniel Lane and Joseph McNally,* District Court, Eighth Judicial District, State of Minnesota.

173 "Mrs. Al Anfinson": *Chokio Review,* May 31, 1962, p. 3, 4.

174 "Order of Distribution": Jim [James P. Kirwin] to Sis [Ruthmary Logue], October 7, 1962, with enclosed order of distribution, 1962, *Kirwin v Lane and McNally* (copy) and "Mae Kirwin Estate, Payments" list, family papers.

176 Dan Lane was seventy: *Ortonville Independent,* December 29, 1982, Section 1, p. 6.

181 "Song in Killeshandra": in *Discriminating Evidence,* 66.

SOURCES

(Sources that provided general background, rather than specific information, are marked with an asterisk.)

Books and Articles

Adams, Mildred. *The American Legion Auxiliary: A History: 1934–1944.* Indianapolis: American Legion Auxiliary, 1945.

Alm, Marlys. "Neither Rain, nor Sleet, nor Snow." In *An Honest Day's Work: Occupations and Enterprises of the Past in Stevens County.* Morris, Minn.: Stevens County Historical Society, 1992. P. 104–6.

Auerbach, Laura K. *Worthy to Be Remembered: A Political History of the Minnesota Democratic-Farmer-Labor Party, 1944–1984.* Minneapolis: Democratic-Farmer-Labor Party of Minnesota, [1984].

Blegen, Theodore C. *Minnesota: A History of the State.* 1963. Reprint. Minneapolis: University of Minnesota Press, 1975.

*Blew, Mary Clearman. *All But the Waltz: A Memoir of Five Generations in the Life of a Montana Family.* New York: Viking Penguin, 1992.

Busch, Edna Mae. *The History of Stevens Co.* [Donnelly?, Minn.]: The Author, [c1976].

Candaele, Kelly, and Kerry Candaele. "Revisionists and the Writing of Irish History." *Irish America,* July–August 1994, p. 22–27.

*Chesler, Phyllis. *Women and Madness.* 1972. Reprint. San Diego: Harcourt Brace Jovanovich, 1989.

Coady, Michael. "Oven Lane: The Use of Memory." *Eire-Ireland* 25 (Winter 1990): 18–33.

Dorweiler, Ann S. *Chokio Community History, 1898–1973.* [Minn.: s.n., 1973?].

*Duncan, Dayton. *Miles from Nowhere: Tales from America's Contemporary Frontier.* New York: Viking, 1993.

*Eagleton, Terry. "Feeding off History." *Observer Magazine,* February 20, 1994, p. 42–44.

Edwards, R. Dudley, and T. Desmond Williams, eds. *The Great Famine: Studies in Irish History, 1845–52.* Dublin: Browne & Nolan for the Irish Committee of Historical Sciences, 1956; New York: New York University Press, 1957.

Glazier, Ira A., ed. *The Famine Immigrants: Lists of Irish Immigrants Arriving at the Port of New York, 1846–1851.* Vol. 4. *April 1849–September 1849.* Baltimore: Genealogical Publishing Co., 1984.

Greeley, Andrew M. *That Most Distressful Nation: The Taming of the American Irish.* Chicago: Quadrangle Books, 1972.

*Grob, Gerald N. *The Mad among Us: A History of the Care of America's Mentally Ill.* New York: Free Press, 1994.

Grubb, Eugene H. *The Potato: A Compilation of Information from Every Available Source.* The Farm Library. Garden City, N.Y.: Doubleday, Page & Co., 1912.

Heilbrun, Carolyn G. "Dorothy L. Sayers: Biography between the Lines." In *Dorothy L. Sayers: The Centenary Celebration,* ed. Alzina Stone Dale. New York: Walker & Co., 1993. P. 2–13.

Holmquist, June Drenning, ed. *They Chose Minnesota: A Survey of the State's Ethnic Groups.* St. Paul: Minnesota Historical Society Press, 1981.

An Honest Day's Work: Occupations and Enterprises of the Past in Stevens County. Morris, Minn.: Stevens County Historical Society, 1992.

Hudson, Lois Phillips. *Reapers of the Dust: A Prairie Chronicle.* Boston: Little, Brown & Co., 1965. Reprint. St. Paul: Minnesota Historical Society Press, Borealis Books, 1984.

Hughes, Thomas. *History of Blue Earth County, and Biographies of Its Leading Citizens.* Chicago: Middle West Publishing Co., [1909?].

Logue, Mary. *Discriminating Evidence: Poems.* Denver: Mid-List Press, 1990.

Lundin, Vernard E. *At the Bend in the River: An Illustrated History of Mankato and North Mankato.* Chatsworth, Calif.: Windsor Publications, 1990.

*Madson, John. "Grandfather Country." *Audubon,* May 1982, p. 40–57.

Mahoney, Rosemary. *Whoredom in Kimmage: Irish Women Coming of Age.* Boston: Houghton Mifflin, 1993.

McCullough, David G., ed. *The American Heritage Picture History of World War II.* New York: American Heritage Publishing Co., 1966.

McGrath, Thomas. *The Bread of this World; Praises III.* St. Paul: Midnight Paper Sales Press, 1992.

*Millett, Kate. *The Loony-Bin Trip.* New York: Simon & Schuster, 1990.

Moley, Raymond, Jr. *The American Legion Story.* New York: Duell, Sloan & Pearce, 1966.

Morison, Samuel Eliot. *History of United States Naval Operations in World War II.* Vol. 12. *Leyte, June 1944–January 1945.* Boston: Little, Brown & Co., 1961.

National Almanac and Year-Book for 1926, ed. James Langland. Chicago: Chicago Daily News, 1926.

O'Neill, Thomas P. "The Organisation and Administration of Relief, 1845–52." In *The Great Famine: Studies in Irish History, 1845–52,* edited by R. Dudley Edwards and T. Desmond Williams. Dublin: Browne & Nolan for the Irish Committee of Historical Sciences, 1956. New York: New York University Press, 1957; p. 209–59.

Patera, Alan H., and John S. Gallagher. *The Post Offices of Minnesota.* Burtonsville, Md.: The Depot, 1978.

Peterson, Emma. "The Geography and Natural History of Stevens County." *Morris Tribune,* June 6, 1903, p. 2.

Prosser, Richard S. *Rails to the North Star.* Minneapolis: Dillon Press, 1966.

Riggs, Stephen Return, ed. *Grammar and Dictionary of the Dakota Language.* Washington City: Smithsonian Institution; New York: G. P. Putnam, 1852.

*Rodgers, Joann Ellison. *Psychosurgery: Damaging the Brain to Save the Mind.* New York: HarperCollins, 1992.

Shannon, James P. *Catholic Colonization on the Western Frontier.* New Haven, Conn.: Yale University Press, 1957.

Thompson, Vye Smeigh, comp. *History: National American Legion Auxiliary.* [Pittsburgh: Jackson-Remlinger Printing Co., 1926].

Tweton, D. Jerome. *Depression: Minnesota in the Thirties.* Fargo: North Dakota Institute for Regional Studies, 1981.

*Wiemers, Amy J. "Rural Irishwomen: Their Changing Role, Status, and Condition." *Eire-Ireland* 29 (Spring 1994): 76–91.

*Wittke, Carl. *The Irish in America*. Baton Rouge: Louisiana State University Press, 1956.

*Woodham-Smith, Cecil. *The Great Hunger: Ireland 1845–49*. London: Hamish Hamilton, 1962; New York: Harper & Row, 1962.

Wulff, Lydia Sorensen. *Big Stone County History*. [Ortonville, Minn.: L. A. Kaercher], 1959.

Wyman, Mark. *Immigrants in the Valley: Irish, Germans, and Americans in the Upper Mississippi Country, 1830–1860*. Chicago: Nelson-Hall, 1984.

Yeats, W. B. *The Collected Poems of W. B. Yeats*. Definitive Edition. New York: Macmillan Publishing Co., 1956.

Newspapers

Blue Earth Post
Bronson Budget
Chokio Review
Chokio Times
Graceville Enterprise
Mankato Free Press
Morris Sun
Morris Tribune
Northern Star (Graceville)
Ortonville Independent
Republican Times (Morris)
Winnebago City Press-News

Manuscript Collections

American Legion Auxiliary, Chokio Post 629. Records. Chokio.

Death records. Stevens County Courthouse. Morris.

Family papers. Members of both the Kirwin and McNally families have collated copies of papers relating to their family histories into large manuscripts. Documents include wills, naturalization papers, school records, death records, and court records.

McNally, Irene. Medical record. Fergus Falls Regional Treatment Center. Fergus Falls.

Maps

Andreas, A. T. An Illustrated Historical Atlas of the State of Minnesota. Chicago: The Author, 1874. Reprint. Evansville, Ind.: Unigraphic, 1976.

Standard Atlas of Stevens County, Minnesota. Chicago: Geo. A. Ogle & Co., 1910.

Government Documents

Minnesota. State Planning Agency. Office of State Demographer. *Population Notes,* April 1991.

U.S. Bureau of the Census. *1987 Census of Agriculture. Volume 1, Geographic Area Series. Part 23, Minnesota State and County Data.* Washington, D.C.: U.S. Dept. of Commerce, Bureau of the Census, [1989].

___. *United States Census of Agriculture, 1925. Minnesota. Statistics by Counties. Final Figures.* Washington, D.C.: GPO, 1928.

___. Post Office Dept. "Record of Appointment of Postmasters, Minnesota, 1832–1971." Microfilm; collections of the Minnesota Historical Society, St. Paul.